To Carol, as always

And to the gang at Tommy's:

Lynn Aronson
Mark Aronson
Bill Cavin
Cokie Cavin
Mark Linneman
Pat Sims
Roger Sims
Dick Spelman

A HUNGER IN THE SOUL

A HUNGER
IN THE
SOUL

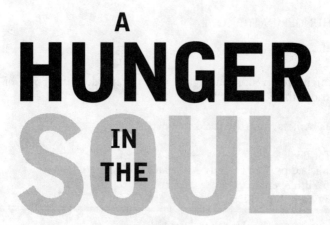

MIKE RESNICK

TOR®

A TOM DOHERTY ASSOCIATES BOOK
NEW YORK

This is a work of fiction. All the characters and events portrayed in this novel are either fictitious or are used fictitiously.

A HUNGER IN THE SOUL

This book is printed on acid-free paper.

A Tor Book
Published by Tom Doherty Associates, LLC
175 Fifth Avenue
New York, NY 10010

Tor Books on the World Wide Web:
www.tor.com

Tor® is a registered trademark of Tom Doherty Associates, LLC

Library of Congress Cataloging-in-Publication Data

Resnick, Michael D.
    A hunger in the soul / Mike Resnick.
        p.   cm.
    "A Tom Doherty Associates Book."
    ISBN 0-312-85438-2 (hc)
    ISBN 0-312-86918-5 (pbk)
    I. Title.
  PS3568.E698H86   1998
  813'.54—dc21   98-5552
                                                          CIP

First Hardcover Edition: May 1998
First Trade Paperback Edition: August 1999

Printed in the United States of America

0 9 8 7 6 5 4 3 2 1

A
HUNGER
IN THE
SOUL

1

Take it from me, there's nothing as annoying as the maniacal giggling of a Sillyworm. It's a cross between a bird screeching, metal rubbing against metal, and an overweight soprano who's been goosed.

Yeah, I know: it sounds amusing. Well, let me tell you, there's nothing amusing about it when three of the damned things are just down the hall from your office, giggling their heads off, while you're trying to concentrate on a job you weren't thrilled with in the first place.

So I stared at the rows of numbers on the computer's screen, which didn't make all that much sense on *good* days, and dreamed of the expeditions I'd never get to lead and the worlds I'd never get to see, and tried not to listen to the Sillyworms—and finally I just turned to the doorway and screamed *"Shut up!"* at the top of my voice.

"I haven't said a word yet," replied the man who was standing there, smiling at me.

I stared at him. He was never going to be a holo star. He stood maybe five feet eight inches, five-nine on his tiptoes, and couldn't have weighed 150 pounds dripping wet. He had a crooked nose, an untrimmed mustache, and a shock of brown hair that needed cutting or combing or both.

"Who the hell are you?" I demanded.

"My name is Robert Horatio Markham," he said, flipping a business card on my desk. It changed colors, and displayed a progression of newstape and magazine headlines.

"Okay, so you're a journalist," I said. "I never heard of you."

"You have that in common with most of the galaxy," he said wryly. Suddenly his smile vanished. "It's a situation that I intend to change. May I sit down, Mr. Stone?"

"Is this going to take long?"

"As long as it has to."

I shrugged and gestured toward a chair; anything was preferable to endless columns of numbers. "Be my guest."

The giggling seemed to grow louder.

"Is there any way you can shut those things up?" he asked. "Feed them, perhaps?"

I laughed. "They're dead, Mr. Markham."

"I don't like being the butt of a joke, Mr. Stone."

"Don't take my word for it," I said. "Go see for yourself." And added mentally, *You touchy son of a bitch.*

He got up, walked down the corridor to inspect the twelve-foot-long creatures, and returned a moment later.

"They're dead," he said, surprised.

"I know."

"Then how can they keep making those noises?"

"That's why they're called Sillyworms," I told him. "Shoot them with a laser or a bullet, or kill them with toxic gas, they act like any other dead animal—but kill them with an ultrasonic weapon and it sets up a sympathetic vibration deep within them

that causes the corpses to giggle maniacally for months, sometimes years."

"Amazing!"

"That pair was taken by Nicobar Lane," I continued. "He's
one of the most famous hunters on the Inner Frontier." And
one of the least grateful. Despite all the business I'd thrown his
way, the bastard never once offered to take me out on safari
after my accident.

"Yes, I know," said Markham. "He's the man who recommended you."

"Recommended me for what?"

"I'm equipping an expedition to Bushveld. I want you to
join me."

"I've already got a job," I said.

"Mr. Lane suggested that it is not a job you enjoy."

"Whether or not I enjoy my job is none of Mr. Lane's business," I said heatedly. So okay, maybe Lane wasn't such a cold-
hearted bastard after all.

"It certainly isn't," he agreed. Then: "Do you?"

I stared at him for a long moment. "I've been the first Man
to set down on forty-three different worlds," I said at last, ges-
turing to the display cases that held the artifacts I'd brought
back for my office collection, artifacts that *should* have made me
as famous as Nicobar Lane. "I've seen lakes and mountains and
deserts no one else has seen to this day. I've brought back half
the animals that are mounted in this goddamned museum and
half the artifacts that are on display. So what do *you* think?"

"Well, then?" said Markham. "Come away with me."

"I'd love to," I said. Then I sighed deeply, as I decided to tell
him the truth. "But you don't want me."

"Why not?"

"My health's shot."

"You look healthy enough to me."

"Look, Mr. Markham," I said. "I lost my left leg on my last

expedition. I still come down with jungle fever every few weeks. I can't pass a physical, and the museum can no longer get insurance on any expedition I lead." I paused. "They were good enough to offer me a position on the staff here," I added, hoping the bitterness didn't show through.

"I don't give a damn about insurance," he said. "I'm on a quest that will make our reputations. Whatever the museum is paying you, I'll triple it."

"And if I can't keep up, or I get sick?" I asked.

"I'll ship you home if it's possible, or leave you behind if it's not." He stared at me. "We all take risks. The money is mine. That's yours."

"Just what are you hunting for?" I asked, trying not to look too enthusiastic.

"The biggest prize of all," he said, his face glowing with excitement. "I'm going out after Michael Drake! I want you to come with me."

"*The* Michael Drake?" I repeated, suddenly deflated. *It had sounded so good. Why the hell did he have to be a crackpot?* "Why not go after the Holy Grail or King Solomon's Mines while you're at it?"

"We don't need them. We need Michael Drake."

"Not unless you want the gold from his fillings," I said. "The man's been dead for years."

"The man's *presumed* dead," responded Markham. "That's not the same thing." He paused. "Michael Drake is the man who developed the ybonia vaccine."

"Every schoolchild knows that."

"Well, what you may not know is that fifteen years ago a mutated form of ybonia broke out in the Belladonna Cluster, and since then it has spread to more than three hundred worlds."

"I'm sorry to hear it, but that doesn't change anything."

"Let me finish," he said sharply. "This new mutation is a

multi-species disease, the only one we've come across so far. It affects Men, Canphorites, and Domarians, and it's highly contagious. That's why Michael Drake went to Bushveld in the first place—to try to come up with a cure for it."

"And since then, nobody's heard from him," I interrupted. "What makes you think he's still alive?"

"Your pal Lane," he said. "He was hunting Hooktooths on Bushveld a few years ago and heard stories of a white-haired man living there, gathering specimens."

"And he says it was Drake?" I asked.

"Lane spends all his time hunting on alien worlds," answered Markham. "He doesn't even know who Michael Drake *is*. But who else could it be?"

"Any botanist or entymologist. Michael Drake doesn't have a monopoly on scientific curiosity." I looked across my desk at him. "How many years ago did Lane hear about this?"

"Maybe five." Markham stared at me. "Well, Mr. Stone, what do you say?"

"Lane was unquestionably your first choice," I noted. "Why did he turn you down?"

"I didn't ask him."

Little bells went off inside my head.

"Something's wrong here," I said. "He's the best hunter in this sector. I'm a has-been with a prosthetic leg. Why am *I* your first choice?"

"He's booked up for the next four years," answered Markham bluntly. At least he wasn't as dumb as I'd feared; the only reason he hadn't offered the job to Nicobar Lane is because he knew he couldn't get him for at least four years—and leaving aside all considerations of whether Michael Drake could last that long *if* he was still alive, I didn't have to be a telepath to know that Markham wasn't willing to wait four years. "Besides," he added, "Lane's a hunter. He kills things. I don't need a killer; I need a guide."

*And he's more famous than you are, and you wouldn't like that
a bit, would you?*

Still, it was a chance to feel the wind of an alien world
against my face once more, a chance that might never come
again. His explanations were too simple and I had a feeling he
was more devious than he appeared, but the alternative was sitting in this office and doping out costs until I retired or went
crazy, and I knew which was liable to happen first.

"Well?" he said. "Are you interested?"

"Yes, I'm interested," I replied. "Anything that will get me
off this planet interests me. But I've got some questions. For ex-
ample: If Drake's alive, why hasn't he contacted anyone with his
ship's radio?"

"Maybe it's not working."

"There are human outposts on Bushveld. He could have
sent a runner."

"Perhaps he did," answered Markham. "How many species
of carnivore are there on Bushveld?"

"Ten or eleven, I can't remember which."

"So maybe one of them ate his runner."

"Maybe," I agreed. "And maybe the man Lane heard about
isn't Michael Drake."

"All the more reason for you to come with me," said
Markham firmly. "I checked you out thoroughly, Mr. Stone.
You've explored more worlds in the Belladonna Cluster than
anyone else, and if Michael Drake has left Bushveld and gone
farther into the Cluster, I need someone who's acquainted with
at least *some* of the worlds where he might have gone." He
paused again. "What do you say?"

He knew the right buttons to push, I'll give him that. I could
only come up with one more question.

"If Drake is the only man who can cure the epidemic, why
hasn't the Democracy gone after him?"

"Three reasons," answered Markham. "First, they think he's

dead. Second, other men are working on a cure; Michael Drake may be the *best* hope, but he's not the only one. And third, all anyone knows for sure is that he vanished on Bushveld years ago. There are eighty thousand worlds in the Belladonna Cluster. If he's alive, he could be on any one of them. The Democracy can't afford the manpower or the money to do the kind of thorough search guaranteed to find him."

"But *you* can?"

"Absolutely."

"What makes you think so?"

"Because I'm sure he's alive. That means I'll search more thoroughly and more vigorously than the Democracy, which is sure he's dead." His smug smile vanished. "And I'll find him."

"When do you plan to leave?" I asked.

"How about tomorrow?"

"Out of the question," I said. "We can't equip an expedition that quickly."

"Why not? We can hire all the help we need once we get to Bushveld."

"Bushveld's a totally undeveloped world," I said. "There probably aren't two hundred Men on it. We're going to have to pick up weaponry, and medical kits, and clothing, and . . ."

"Okay, I get the point."

"Will there be any other Men in the party?" I asked.

"I've hired a pair of holographers to record every aspect of the expedition. They'll be joining us here before we leave."

"What about a doctor?" I asked.

"You think we'll need one?"

"What do *you* think?" I said. "We're going to spend most of our time in a jungle on an alien world. We probably haven't even cataloged the diseases yet, let alone produced vaccines for them."

"Right. We'll add a doctor." He paused. "What else are we going to need before we can begin?"

And suddenly I was making a list for him, and he was costing it out, and I realized that my decision was made. I was actually going back into the Inner Frontier to help a total stranger look for the fabled Michael Drake, who had vanished from the sight and knowledge of men fifteen years ago.

It's amazing what a man will do when presented with the possibility, no matter how remote, of galaxywide fame.

2

It had been a few years since I'd had to equip an expedition, but once I got to work it felt like it had just been yesterday. And the fact that Markham's sponsors seemed to have limitless resources made the job that much easier.

I ordered six climate-controlled collapsible bubbles, each ten feet in diameter, for the Men. There would be Markham, myself, the two cameramen Markham had hired, and Dr. Hiram Wentzel, who had agreed on short notice to shutter his practice and come on the expedition. I felt especially good about that, because Wentzel was the medic who had amputated my gangrenous leg and kept me alive on that disastrous final safari. I had also insisted upon a meat hunter, Kenny Vaughn, whom I had used on my previous trips to Bushveld; one of the tiny handful of Men who'd been born and raised on the planet, he knew the terrain, the animals, the natives, the taboos, and a goodly number of the dialects.

I also laid in a three-month store of soya products for us. It was a compromise. By rights, I should have laid in a year's worth . . . but that would imply that I had no faith in Vaughn. Besides, I *hated* soya products. Soya steak and soya fish always tasted a lot more like processed soybeans than like steak or fish. Still, the hunter and the soya products notwithstanding, I refused to go out with no foodstuffs at all.

The medical kit Wentzel had requested got out of hand early. There were seventeen known diseases that Men could catch in the jungles of Bushveld, but we could also be attacked by any of the numerous species of carnivore. And there was always a chance that Michael Drake had moved on to some other world, so we took as many broad-based antidotes as we could. Dr. Wentzel also insisted on adding a year's supply of adrenaline and blood-oxygenating units to help us overcome the heat and the lower oxygen content of Bushveld's atmosphere.

I knew from prior experience to bring along two refrigeration units: one for the medication, one for the beer and cold drinks. Bring just one, and within weeks the Men would be tossing serums and antibiotics into a nearby swamp to make room for the drinks. (I made a note to check with the cameramen and see if their holodisks needed refrigeration as well.)

I figured Markham had just enough of an ego to want to bring back some trophies other than a living Michael Drake, and I sent a subspace message off to a friend at the museum on Dabih Minor. The blue-skinned humanoid Dabihs were the best skinners on the Frontier, and I didn't want any of the hired help ruining the heads Markham took. I considered getting bubbles for the Dabihs, but finally decided against it; every time I'd employed them, they had preferred sleeping out under the stars, and while I was willing to spend Markham's money, I had no interest in wasting it.

There was a lot of water on Bushveld, but I didn't think we'd spend any time on it. If Drake was there at all, he'd be inland, experimenting with various plants in his search for a cure.

I ordered three safari vehicles, all of which could negotiate water as well as glide above the rough terrain. Cold-fusion engines were too expensive, and too hard to fix when they went on strike in the middle of the bush, so I settled for solar-powered units. I also found a two-man helioplane that broke down to fit inside one of the vehicles and could be reassembled in about twenty minutes, so that we could try to spot his camp from the air. Then I contacted Kipsogi Ngami, the best mechanic I knew, and offered him a year's contract to keep the vehicles working (which meant I then had to go back and lay in another bubble, more food, etc.).

When it came to weapons, I decided that the meat hunter had his own, the photographers didn't need any, and Markham would probably resent my selecting one for him. I unlocked my privacy chest and pulled out some of the tried-and-true weaponry I had used on previous expeditions: a laser rifle, a sonic pistol, a projectile gun, a molecular imploder. I decided to pack the Burner and the Screecher and leave the bullet gun and the imploder behind.

I figured each of the men would bring his own personal kit: shaving equipment, prescribed medications, and the like. I leaned back on my chair, trying to think of what else we would need, what I might be missing. I began making a list: infrared Spy-Eyes; a ton of salt in ten-pound bags for trading with the salt-starved inhabitants of Bushveld; and, finally, half a dozen Vermin Zappers, which would kill any small nasty creature—insect, reptile, mammal, or other—that wandered into camp while leaving all larger life-forms unmolested.

I kept making more lists and ordering more items, and contacted the cameramen to see if they had any special needs. I figured as long as Markham's money held out, I was going to make sure we were prepared for anything we might encounter, except maybe each other.

This Markham guy is pretty well-heeled," commented Kip Ngami, as I showed him around the warehouse where I was storing our supplies. He gestured toward the safari vehicles. "These are state-of-the-art. So is the helioplane."

"His publisher's got deep pockets," I said.

Ngami picked up the Burner. "Does his publisher want to *find* Michael Drake or *shoot* him?"

"That's mine."

"Same question."

"It's a jungle world," I said. "You never know what you might need."

"A molecular imploder will kill anything that bothers you faster and more efficiently than this stuff," he remarked, laying the Burner down next to the Screecher. "Besides," he continued, "you told me you've hired Kenny Vaughn. He's all the protection you'll need."

"Markham's got to send features back almost every day," I said. "He'll send them to the ship, which will beam them back to the Democracy with its subspace transmitter. Until we find Drake, he's going to be hard up for material. I figured maybe he could turn an occasional trophy into a day's story. There's nothing left to mount after you nail it with an imploder."

"What's he like?" asked Ngami.

"I told you," I replied. "He's a journalist."

"I didn't ask what he did. I asked what he's *like*. I've been on safari with *you*, so I know what to expect. I've never even heard of him—and we're going to be working for him for as long as it takes him to find Michael Drake, or at least until he gives up."

"He seems all right," I said. "Nothing special."

"Good."

"What's so good about it?" I asked, puzzled.

"Lord save me from special people."

Markham kept peppering me with communications until I was tempted to deactivate my computer. Finally I sent word that we were ready to leave, and within hours everything—the supplies, the bubbles, the vehicles—had been loaded into a cargo ship that bore the Universal Features Syndicate logo. Markham showed up just before takeoff with his two cameramen. Dr. Wentzel and the two Dabih skinners were to meet us on Bushveld, where Vaughn was arranging for our native help. I had told him to hire as many healthy bodies as he thought we would need, and left the final number up to him.

The inside of the ship was surprising, for while the cargo hold was like every other cargo hold I'd ever seen, the top deck—the living quarters—was as luxurious as the hold was utilitarian. There were couches and chairs, a holographic fireplace with a holographic fire crackling away, a well-stocked kitchen, four private cabins with king-sized airbeds and en-suite bathrooms. Perhaps most luxurious of all, the showers used real water rather than the usual combination of chemicals.

"We'll be *un*comfortable soon enough," explained Markham, leaning back on his chair, which floated inches above the deck, and lighting a smokeless pipe. "No reason why we shouldn't enjoy the comforts of civilization as long as we can."

"Have you ever been on this type of expedition before?" asked Kip Ngami.

"I'm a writer, not an explorer," he said. "Why?"

"I was just wondering how you'll react to nasty insects in your shoes and ugly ones in your coffee and huge ones in your shower," said Kip with a smile.

"I thought we packed a bunch of Vermin Zappers."

"We did—but we'll be covering a lot of territory. You can't zap every inch of it."

"I'll adjust to whatever conditions exist on Bushveld, Mr. Ngami," said Markham confidently. "And I'll do it faster than you or Mr. Stone."

"If you say so," replied Kip skeptically.

Markham turned to me. "Do I strike you as someone who throws in the towel when things get rough?"

I shrugged. "I don't know you well enough to say."

"You will," he said. "And whatever the hardship, you and everyone else will quit—or try to—long before I do."

"It's possible," I said, though I didn't believe it, and I could see from the twinkle in Kip's eye that he didn't buy it either—which just goes to show how much we still had to learn about Robert Markham.

Markham spent most of his waking hours in the lounge, watching holo footage of Michael Drake that he'd acquired from archives all across the Democracy. He didn't insist that anyone else watch it, but it was pretty hard not to if you were anywhere in the room.

The two holographers stayed in their cabins for most of the voyage. Kip Ngami found out that they'd worked for Markham before, and while they admitted he paid well, they didn't seem very anxious to socialize with him.

That left Kip and myself as Markham's only companions for most of the voyage. Drake's entire life kept flashing interminably before our eyes (at least until we, too, began sneaking off to our cabins whenever we could get away with it). The history began with Drake graduating at the top of his class on the university planet of Aristotle. Then came his dalliance with philosophy, culminating in his Fourteen Modest Steps, the only argument for the existence a Judeo-Christian God that had

never been disproved. Most of the footage concerned his cre-
ation of a vaccine for ybonia, which was estimated to have saved
more than thirty billion lives across the Democracy. He refused
all payment or royalties for it; he simply *gave* it to the Democracy
to administer at cost—a fact that seemed to impress Markham
even more than his work on the vaccine. Then there was his
final press conference on Deluros VIII, the huge capital world
of Man, as he prepared to go off to the Inner Frontier in search
of a cure for ybonia A, which was what the mutated virus was
called at the time.

As far as I could tell—and I was not alone in my opinion; an
entire galaxy shared it—Michael Drake was the greatest man of
our era. His only character flaw was an excess of modesty. He
seemed genuinely unaware of the fact that he was, well, *Michael
Drake*.

It made an interesting contrast to Markham, who had his
initials on his boots, his shirts, his luggage, his weapons, his
computer, and—I assumed—his underwear.

But, of course, Markham was out to rescue Drake, not become him.

Have you been listening to him?" asked Ngami, when I went to
the galley with him to get some dinner.

"To Drake?"

"To Markham," he replied.

"All he talks about is Michael Drake," I said. "It's easier to
tune him out."

"Start paying attention," said Ngami. "He's not exactly a
fan."

"I beg your pardon?"

"He sits there looking for flaws. It's not enough that Drake
refused payment for the vaccine; he wants to know *why*. Drake
is so dedicated to his work he never married, so Markham won-

ders if he's a homosexual. It's more like Drake's an opponent he's sizing up rather than a man he's planning to rescue."

"He's a journalist," I said. "Who knows how their minds work? Maybe he's just looking for human foibles to write about."

Ngami grimaced. "I thought journalists were supposed to be perceptive," he said. "Michael Drake is the greatest man of our era. He's a saint."

"He'd damned well better be," said Markham, who had silently joined us. "They're not paying me to drag a sinner out of the bush."

Kip Ngami stormed into my cabin as I was lying on my airbed, reading.

"What's the matter?" I asked.

"You'd better get up to the bridge right away!"

"Why?"

"Your boss is reprogramming the navigational computer!" he said.

"He's *what?*"

"You heard me."

I raced up to the bridge, and found Markham loading in the final coordinates.

"What the hell are you doing?" I demanded.

"Loading in new landing coordinates," he said calmly.

"Put the old ones back," I ordered him.

"Why should I?"

"For one thing, I told Wentzel, Vaughn, and the Dabihs to meet us at Fort Capstick. For another, that's the only Customs and Immigration port on the whole planet."

"We can give them our coordinates once we land."

"We can't start an expedition without clearing customs, and I won't break the law my first day back on Bushveld."

"You're off the hook," he said. "You'll be breaking it on my orders."

"I don't break it for *anyone,*" I said angrily. "Either I'm the leader of this expedition or I'm not. If I'm not, tell me now. The museum will be happy to have me back."

He stared long and hard at me, trying to control his temper. "You're costing me time," he said at last, "and time is the one irreplaceable commodity."

"If Drake's on the planet, he'll have begun his expedition at Fort Capstick," I said. "He may still be in contact with them."

"We know where he was supposed to be when Nicobar Lane was on the planet," replied Markham. "Who cares where he started?"

"We don't know for a fact that the man Lane heard about *was* Drake," I pointed out.

"Yes, we do."

"How?"

"Because I'm the best journalist alive," answered Markham, "and my gut instinct tells me that Drake's where Nicobar Lane said he'd be."

Modest, too, I thought. *Why am I wasting my time working for a smug, pompous asshole like you?* Then I remembered: because no one else would take me away from that goddamned desk in that goddamned museum and give me a shot at something meaningful, something that might justify all the long years I'd spent on the Frontier.

"You disagree?" he persisted.

"It *could* be Drake," I said. "Or it could be an escaped criminal hiding from the law. Or the sole survivor of a shipwreck who doesn't even know what world he's on. Or maybe it's one of those nutcases from Far London who likes to run around in tropical climates with his clothes off."

He looked at me distastefully, as if I were a Far London case myself.

"It's Drake," he announced with absolute conviction.

"I hope so," I said. "But I'm still not going to break the law. He's been missing for more than fifteen years; he can stay missing for an extra day."

He continued staring at me, but finally canceled his orders to the navigational computer. Then he went back to the lounge to watch more holos of Michael Drake.

Later, I would see Robert Markham kill people for displaying far less insubordination than I'd shown. And I would see him tolerate much worse from people he needed, at least while he needed them. But at the moment I didn't give it much thought. After all, I was in charge of the expedition; he was just an undersized and somewhat unpleasant writer that I was going to have to keep alive long enough to make us both rich and famous.

Well, I used to believe in Santa Claus, and the Ghost of Rigel VII, too.

3

I **had almost** forgotten just how hot and muggy Bushveld was. I was forcibly reminded of it about two seconds after I rode the ship's escalator down to the ground and got into an open-air vehicle that took us to the customs desk at the spaceport. I spotted Kenny Vaughn waiting on the other side of a barrier, and waved to him, but I couldn't get close enough to speak to him until we cleared customs.

I thought we'd have some problems. Customs officials— especially on out-of-the-way worlds like Bushveld—tend to be very fussy men and women who want to dot every "i" and cross every "t." But a tall, white-haired gentleman showed up and waved us through.

"Glad to meet you, Mr. Markham," he said, shaking Markham's hand. "I'm Wallace Penner, the governor of Bushveld. I can't tell you how happy we are to have a journalist of your stature visiting us."

Markham practically glowed, but I noticed that he managed

to avoid shaking hands until the cameramen were able to capture it. "It's very kind of you to say so, Governor Penner. I hope
we can do justice to both your hospitality and your lovely world."

"Well, I wouldn't exactly call it *lovely,*" admitted Penner. "It's
a bit of a backwater. But we do the best we can to make the
Democracy's presence felt." He put a friendly arm around
Kenny's shoulders. "Allow me to introduce you to your hunter,
Kenny Vaughn, a true native of Bushveld. We're all very proud
of him."

Markham shook Kenny's hand, and seemed about to say
something when Penner intervened.

"When I heard you were coming to Bushveld, I arranged a
banquet for this evening." He smiled apologetically. "We have
so few occasions to dine elegantly, we relish that handful of
times when it's actually called for." He looked at me and Kip
and the cameramen. "Of course your entire human contingent
is invited."

"I'm afraid we plan on starting our expedition almost immediately," replied Markham.

Penner looked as if he'd just lost his best friend. "But it's all
arranged!"

"And we appreciate it," said Markham. "But why not wait
until we return with Michael Drake? Then we'll have cause for
celebration."

"Then I promise you a triumphal feast the day of your return," agreed Penner enthusiastically. "I'll be happy to do anything I can to help you find him." *And,* his expression seemed
to say, *maybe use it as a passport off this insignificant little world in
the middle of nowhere.* "In the meantime, would you like a tour
of Fort Capstick?" continued Penner. "We'll end it at Government House, where I just happen to have an unopened bottle of
Cygnian cognac."

"That sounds fine," responded Markham. "Would you mind
if my crew captured it for posterity?"

Penner was thrilled: now there would be holographic proof that he had aided and abetted Markham. "Not at all, Mr. Markham," he said. "Not at all."

Markham turned to Arnaz and Kerr, the two cameramen. "Go with the governor and dope out where the best shots are. I'll be along in a few minutes."

As they left, Kenny took a step forward. "Hello, Enoch," he said in his rich, deep voice. "Good to see you again."

"Hello, Kenny," I said. "Where's the rest of our party?"

"The two Dabihs got here yesterday," he answered. "Your medic hasn't shown up yet."

Markham turned to me. *"You* hired him, Mr. Stone."

I summoned one of the spaceport officials. "Have you had any word from Dr. Hiram Wentzel?"

The woman checked her pocket computer. "He radioed that his ship had some mechanical problems and had to put into port. We now expect him tomorrow morning."

Markham turned back to Vaughn. "How soon are we prepared to start?"

"Whenever you want," answered Kenny. "I've made reservations for your party at our best hotel." Suddenly he smiled. "Our *only* hotel, actually. I thought you might like to unwind for a few days after your flight."

"You heard what I told the governor," said Markham. "Our flight was the last luxury we will experience until we get off this ugly little dirtball and return to civilization. We want to begin the expedition as soon as possible."

Vaughn frowned at the insult to his planet and its facilities. Bushveld was, after all, the only civilization he had ever known.

"We can leave this afternoon, if you wish," he replied at last.

"I should be able to finish my duty dance with the governor in less than an hour," said Markham. "Can we be ready to go an hour after that?"

"No reason why not," answered Vaughn.

"How many aliens did you hire?"

"None," said Vaughn, and I could tell he had again taken offense at Markham's manner. "The only two aliens on the expedition will be the Dabih skinners."

"I gave explicit orders that you were to outfit this expedition," said Markham. "Did you misunderstand my instructions?"

"No, sir."

"Then why didn't you hire anyone?"

"I hired fifty *natives*," said Vaughn. "You see, on Bushveld, *Men* are the aliens."

Markham stared at him for a moment, and I got the distinct impression that if he could find another hunter before we left, he'd fire Vaughn. I also knew that he almost certainly couldn't find one on such short notice—and that Vaughn was every bit as capable of walking away right now as Markham was of terminating him. Since I didn't relish an extended diet of soya products and wandering through uncharted wilderness without a guide who knew the languages and the customs, I thought I'd better intervene—but Kip Ngami beat me to the punch.

"How are you doing, Kenny?" he said, stepping forward. "Still blowing away charging Devildogs at six feet?"

Vaughn smiled. "Hi, Kip. I didn't know you'd be coming along. Do you still make reluctant motors purr like one of your ladyfriends?"

"That's what I'm here for," said Kip.

"If the mutual admiration society is through," interrupted Markham, "let's start unloading the ship."

"It's already being unloaded," said Vaughn.

"It is?"

"I told the cargo handlers that you'd double their pay for a quick job."

"You may work out after all, Mr. Vaughn," said Markham.

"I like a man who shows initiative." With that, he turned and walked off to join the governor.

"Sweet guy," said Vaughn, staring after him.

"Can you work with him?" I asked.

"Why not? I'll be alone in the bush most of the time, hunting for your dinner." He smiled. "Can *you* work with him?"

"I hope so," I said. "I quit my job to come here."

"We'll wear him down," said Kip. "A little hiking, a little dysentery, a little this, a little that, he should be almost human in a couple of weeks."

"Nobody's getting sick," I said. "That's why we're bringing Wentzel along."

"He's history," said Kip. "Didn't you hear Markham? We're leaving in two hours."

"So he'll catch up with us."

Kip pulled a banknote out of his pocket. "Fifty New Stalin rubles says Markham fires him before he has a chance to join us."

"Why the hell would he do that?" I said, pulling out a two-hundred-credit note.

"Because he *can*," answered Kip.

"He could have fired Kenny, too—but he didn't."

"There's a difference."

"What?" I demanded.

"If he fires Kenny, he has to recruit fifty natives himself," said Kip. "It could take him weeks. If he fires Hiram Wentzel, we've still got all the medical supplies that Wentzel told you to bring."

"They won't do much good if someone breaks a leg, or gets mauled by a Silverfang."

"True," agreed Kip, smiling. "Do we have a bet?"

I handed my note to Vaughn. "You hold it," I said, and Kip turned his money over as well.

"I suppose I'd better go round up our natives," said Vaughn.

"Before you do . . ." I said.

"Yes?"

"*Somebody* ought to ask the question, and it doesn't seem to have occurred to Markham," I continued. "Has anyone in Fort Capstick seen or heard from Michael Drake?"

Vaughn shook his head. "Since Nicobar Lane was here, you mean? No." He began walking away. "I'll meet you here at 1300 hours."

"Fine," I said, and then realized that I didn't know the local time. "What is it now?"

He looked at his watch. "1040 hours."

"And how many Standard hours in a Bushveld day?" I asked, trying unsuccessfully to remember.

"2635."

"All right," I said, reprogramming my watch. "We'll be here."

"Well," said Kip after Vaughn had left, "I don't know about you, but I'm starved. I saw a restaurant across from the spaceport. Care to give it a try?"

"Why not?" I said.

We strolled over to it and were seated immediately. After we ordered our food, I looked out the window and saw Markham and Penner, maybe fifty yards away, posing on the stairs of Government House and beaming at the cameras.

"They look like they've hit it off," I commented.

"They're probably busy picking each other's pockets," replied Kip. He smiled sardonically. "I notice he didn't ask us to join him."

"I'd rather eat," I said. "Besides, we're not here to get photographed with the governor."

"I know why *I'm* here. I'm still wondering why you are."

"Because it's not a small room on the third floor of a museum," I replied.

"You really think you're going to grab the brass ring this time?"

I shrugged. "Who knows?"

Our food arrived just then. The waiter was an Orange-Eye, a member of the humanoid race that had reached the top of Bushveld's evolutionary ladder. He was about five feet tall, with two orange eyes, a pair of slits for nostrils, an ample mouth, large cupped ears, broad powerful shoulders, oddly jointed arms and fingers, and exceptionally long legs that could carry him effortlessly across vast expanses of ground. The waiter's outfit hid his skin, but I knew that it was covered with orange fur that thickened during the rains and shed out during the dry season.

He said something that I couldn't quite understand. After two repetitions, I figured out that he was asking if we wanted our coffee sweetened, and I realized it was going to take a few days for my ear to adjust to the thickly accented Terran that the Orange-Eyes spoke. (In almost a year on the planet, I'd only picked up about thirty words of one of their dialects, which consisted primarily of grunts, chirps, and glottal clicks.)

After we'd eaten, Kip and I decided to take a quick tour of Fort Capstick. The entire colony covered less than thirty acres. There was Government House, of course, and the spaceport. The town had only one hotel, small and whitewashed, hopefully with a more comfortable bed than it possessed during my last trip here. Next door to it was a bar with a couple of slowly spinning ceiling fans; a trio of men were sipping beers on a shaded terrace. I assumed they were tourists, but they just as easily could have been expatriates. There was a weapons shop, which specialized in sporting guns and pistols, and had a large sign in the window stating that they did not handle molecular imploders and magna pulse rifles. Tucked away on a tiny street behind Government House were a taxidermist, a map shop, a dry-goods store, and a catchall shop that sold everything else a human could want, from toothpaste to medications to the chemical Dryshowers that came in so handy on the safari trail.

"It sure hasn't changed much, has it?" remarked Kip.

"It's too far off the beaten track to attract many tourists." I replied, wiping some sweat off my forehead. "I'll bet the hotel hasn't been completely full since Johnny Ramsey left office and went on that hunting trip that took him all across the Inner Frontier."

"I always wondered how he managed to sneak up on anything," said Kip with a laugh. "The man was always surrounded by a couple of hundred newsmen and biographers. Kind of like Markham writ big."

"Markham's not sneaking up on anything," I pointed out. "He's trying to find Michael Drake, and the more Men and Orange-Eyes who know about it, the better his chance—*our* chance—of success." I paused. "We'll leave the shooting to Kenny Vaughn."

"Markham opens his mouth too many more times, Kenny might just consider having *him* stuffed and mounted."

"As Kenny himself pointed out, he'll hardly ever be in camp," I noted.

"Just the same," said Kip, "if I was Markham and I had to stay on friendly terms with just one member of this expedition, I'd choose the man with the gun."

There wasn't much more to see of the colony, and the heat had become oppressive, so we wandered back to the spaceport. Most of our Orange-Eyes had already gathered there. They stared silently at us as we walked by. Most of them were either totally naked, or clad in a gold-and-brown animal skin that was wrapped around their waists and descended almost to the ground.

I looked over at the ship. Markham had returned from Government House and was now supervising the unloading of the safari vehicles.

"I suppose I'd better go over there and make sure the plane's working," remarked Kip with an unhappy sigh.

"Can you do it alone?" I asked.

"I need some muscle to help hold parts of it steady while I'm making the connections," he answered. "I'll grab a couple of Orange-Eyes."

He walked over to the crowd of Orange-Eyes and appropriated two of them to help him. It took him less than fifteen minutes to assemble the little helioplane. As he finished testing the motor, Markham came over to see what his flying machine looked like and nodded his approval. It took Kip about five minutes to break it down again and load it into the back of a safari vehicle.

"Let's get something cold to drink," said Kip, returning to my side. "I'm not used to this pea soup."

Vaughn showed up with the rest of the crew about an hour later, and Markham announced that we would leave immediately, the Orange-Eyes to march behind the vehicles until we left the savannah and reached the jungle, where they would use their long, vicious knives to break the trail.

I left our radio frequency for Wentzel, so he could contact us when he arrived. Then Markham and I climbed into the first safari vehicle, the cameramen shared the second, and Kip got to ride alone in the third. Vaughn, driving his own beat-up vehicle and accompanied by the two blue-skinned Dabihs, had already vanished into the bush, more to keep away from Markham than to hunt for game during the heat of the day, when it was least likely to be up and around.

We were less than four miles out of Fort Capstick when we came to a herd of Landwhales, huge herbivores some twenty feet at the shoulder, with thick, layered, brown skin. They were grazing placidly, and paid no attention to the vehicles or the accompanying Orange-Eyes.

"Stop!" said Markham excitedly.

I thought he wanted Arnaz and Kerr to photograph these peaceful giants, but before I realized what he was doing he'd pulled his Screecher out of its protective jacket and fired point-blank at a female Landwhale who had a young calf trailing behind her. She shrieked, spun around two or three times, and then collapsed, her feet twitching spasmodically. The calf stood beside her, whining piteously, while the rest of the herd milled about in confusion and then ponderously ran off, bellowing in fear.

Markham jumped out of the vehicle, climbed onto the dead Landwhale, and waited while Arnaz carried his camera over to capture the triumphant moment for posterity. A moment later he was back on his seat, and we started moving again, leaving the dead Landwhale and her helpless calf behind.

The expedition was less than twenty minutes old, and already I envied Kenny Vaughn.

4

We drove slowly through the savannah until late afternoon, then stopped to set up a temporary camp. (The only real difference between a temporary camp and a permanent one is that you don't prepare shelters for your vehicles or larders for your meat, since you plan to be leaving in the morning.)

Vaughn showed up just as the Orange-Eyes had finished setting up our portable bubbles and were working on the mess area, which was really nothing but a force field above the table at which the Men would be sitting. Once the Treeswingers discovered that it would support their weight, they spent the rest of the evening racing across it, even though they couldn't see it.

Vaughn had killed two small grass-eaters, about eighty pounds apiece, and dropped them off for our Orange-Eye chef to cook. Since this was our first night on safari, he made sure the chef understood which cuts of meat to keep for the Men (tenderloin and sirloin), and which to give to his fellow Orange-Eyes (everything else).

Next, he ordered a couple of Orange-Eyes to take his bubble down.

"What's the problem?" I asked. "Markham hasn't had a chance to get you mad yet."

"He hasn't said a word to me since I arrived," replied Vaughn. "And I consider that a healthy relationship. I plan to set up my own camp elsewhere. I'll check in every day with your meat supply. Fifty of these Orange-Eye boys should take a hundred and fifty pounds a day, and the Men should be good for another ten pounds."

"You call them boys?" I asked.

"Twenty years from now they'll probably want to lynch me for it, but no one's raised their consciousness yet," said Vaughn. Suddenly he chuckled. "Besides, I *can't* call them 'boy' in their own language. There's no word for it."

"I wish you'd stick around," I said.

"To protect you from the beasts of the jungle or the beast of journalism?" he asked.

"To act as a go-between with the Orange-Eyes," I said. "After all, you're the only one here who speaks their dialect . . . and you've spent your entire life on this planet, so you should know how to get along with them."

"They're hard workers, and they're incapable of lying," replied Vaughn. "Big Shoulders and Cotton Jacket speak pretty good Terran, and a few of the others can at least understand simple orders without a translating mechanism. Just tell 'em what to do, and try not to work them too hard, since this expedition could last more than a year and you don't want to lose any of them. As for getting along with them . . . it's their job to get along with *you*."

"I still wish you'd stay in camp."

He grinned. "I'll bet you do."

"He's your employer too, you know," I said, a bit sullenly.

"I'm doing my job," answered Vaughn. "And my job doesn't include listening to him. All I'm being paid to do is feed him and tell him where to go—or, at least, where *not* to go."

"Thanks a lot."

"Any time, Enoch old friend," he said, still smiling. He hefted his rifle, said something I couldn't understand to the Dabihs, and headed off into the bush.

"Too bad all he has to kill are Landwhales and Demoncats and the like," remarked Kip, "rather than something truly formidable, like, say, Robert Markham."

"Who'd pay you, then?" I asked.

"I hate it when you ask questions like that," said Kip with a smile.

I decided it was time for the expedition leader—me—to get to work. Markham was busy dictating into his pocket computer and posing for holographs, so I spent the last hour of daylight checking out the camp. I saw to it that the five bubbles were lined up in a row, each facing the nearby river, so that we could see the animals coming down to drink. I made sure the Dryshowers were operating properly, ordered a couple of Orange-Eyes to dig a pit where we would bury the inserts from our Sani-toilets, and saw that the water from the nearby stream was properly sanitized. These were all routine chores, and Big Shoulders—that was the name Vaughn had given to our Orange-Eye headman—could just as easily have seen to them, but it kept me busy, and more to the point, it kept me away from Markham.

Eventually, though, the day ended, night fell, and we had to eat, so the five Men sat down in the mess area, well away from the Orange-Eyes, who had set up their own camp a few hundred yards to the south and were singing songs as they cooked their meat over an open fire until it was almost black.

"A very dull first day," remarked Markham.

"You mean we weren't attacked or eaten," said Kip.

"I mean I have nothing worthwhile to transmit back to the ship," answered Markham.

"You blew away a Landwhale," said Kip. "Doesn't that count for something?"

"That was my noontime story. I'm trying to do two features a day." Markham suddenly looked around the camp. "Where is the estimable Mr. Vaughn?"

"He's camped a few miles away," I answered.

"Why?"

"Most of the game is up and moving at sunrise, and that's the best time to go after it," I explained, relieved that I was able to give him a truthful answer, if not *the* truth. "Our camp is so large and so noisy that the herbivores are giving it a wide berth. Kenny saves himself a lot of stalking time by starting out where they live, rather than hoping he leaves camp in the right direction to find one of the herds."

"Makes sense," acknowledged Markham. He peered into the darkness. "But I still need two features a day."

"I wouldn't count on getting them," I said. "Most of the days are going to be pretty dull. They'll consist of following one false trail after another until we finally luck out and find Michael Drake—or prove to our satisfaction that he's not alive or not on Bushveld, or both."

"Your job is to guide the expedition," said Markham. "Mine is to come up with features. I don't have the skills to run the expedition"—the word *yet* seemed to hover in the air—"and you don't have the skills to be a successful journalist." *And no one as stupid as you ever will* was the implication.

"Go easy on him, Mr. Markham," said Kerr, one of the cameramen. "He didn't mean any offense."

"I know he didn't," said Markham irritably.

"Then be a little less belligerent," Kip said.

"Me, belligerent?" he repeated, genuinely surprised. "That's the silliest thing I ever heard!"

He downed a huge cannister of beer and then marched off to his bubble, probably to use the Sani-toilet.

"Him, belligerent?" muttered Kip. "Perish the thought!"

Arnaz uttered an amused chuckle.

"You guys have worked with him before," continued Kip, turning to the cameramen. "What could possibly make you willing to put up with him a second time?"

"It's a seventh time for me," said Kerr.

"And a third for me," added Arnaz.

"Why?"

"Because he's as good as he says he is," answered Kerr seriously. "I want my work to be noticed. There's no better way than to be the cameraman for a Markham documentary or supply the still holos in a Markham book." He paused. "Besides, he's not so bad once you get used to him. He demands perfection—but he demands it of himself, too. And he delivers. Read some of his stuff someday."

"Okay, he's a brilliant writer," continued Kip. "But that still doesn't explain how you can put up with all the shit."

"View it as being an athlete," said Kerr. "You'll put up with all kinds of abuse from your coach if you know he's making you better all the time. Well, working with Markham makes you better."

"How?" asked Kip. "He's a writer, you're a holographer. He just tells you what to aim your camera at, and that's it."

"He demands the best shots, the best angles, the best lighting, the best cuts," answered Kerr. "And when he tells you how to get them, where you fucked up and where you can improve, it doesn't matter how abrasive he is. The point is that he's *right*, and you learn from it."

"I'd be ready to kill him after seven expeditions," said Kip. "Hell, I'll probably be ready three days into my first one."

Kerr smiled. "I feel that way myself sometimes. But then I look at my work before I started going out with him, and I look at what I'm producing now, and suddenly I remember why I put up with him."

A family of golden-haired Treeswingers took up residence in a tree about thirty feet above us, chattering happily and looking down and studying us the way we might look down and study insects.

"How about you?" asked Kip, turning to Arnaz, the smaller of the two holographers. "Are you in it for self-improvement too?"

Arnaz shook his head. "I hate that bastard. Someday I'll probably kill him."

"So why do you come back?"

"I make more money from him than from anyone else," answered Arnaz, glancing up as one of the Treeswingers in the branches above our heads began shrieking for no discernible reason. "I mean, hell, everyone talks about finding Michael Drake, but Markham is the only journalist who's got a major syndicate to back him and pick up all his expenses. My own guess is that Drake has been dead for years . . . but if we *do* find him, I'm going to make enough to retire at age thirty-eight."

"And if we don't find him?"

Arnaz shrugged. "Then," he said thoughtfully, "if I don't kill him first, I'll follow Markham on his next wild-goose chase and make enough to retire at forty."

"So he's really that good?" I mused.

"What are you doing here if you didn't believe his credentials?" asked Kerr as a Hooktooth roared in the distance.

"I believed his money and his possibilities," I answered. "And he got me out of my goddamned office."

"You couldn't leave your office without him?"

I rolled up my pants leg and showed off my perfect left leg. "Prosthetic?" asked Kerr.

I nodded.

"When did you lose it?"

"My last expedition," I said.

"He traded his leg for his client's life," added Kip.

"Sounds like there's a hell of a story here," said Kerr, leaning forward.

"Only in retrospect," I said. "And only if you weren't the guy who lost the leg."

"You're not going to tell us how you lost it?" persisted Kerr.

"I think one hero at a time is about all we can handle," I said as Markham emerged from his bubble and rejoined our little group, taking his seat at the head of the table.

"I heard something screech a moment ago," he said. "Does anyone know what it was?"

"I'm not in Kenny Vaughn's class as an avian expert," I replied, "but I do know that Bushveld has twenty-three species of raptor, nine of which are nocturnal. My guess is that it was a Nightdiver."

"Why that species rather than one of the others?" asked Markham.

"Because they scream to startle their prey into an instant of immobility, which is usually enough."

"Fascinating," said Markham. "So I heard a Nightdiver making a kill?"

"No," I corrected him. "You heard it just prior to making— or losing—a kill. It grabs its prey with its claws and kills with a razor-sharp beak, so it couldn't very well voice that cry while it was in the act of killing."

"I think that's worth a feature," said Markham. "I just may pick Mr. Vaughn's mind and see if he can help us get some footage of it."

His presence wasn't exactly a boon to conversation. We all fell silent, and one by one we walked over to the fire, warming ourselves and staring into the dancing flames. Finally Markham

realized that he had been deserted. He opened a bottle of
Denebian whisky, which is about as upscale as you can get, took
a healthy swig, then joined us at the campfire and passed the
bottle around. Everyone partook except Kerr.

"Good stuff," said Kip.

"Made in the vineyards on Deneb IV," said Markham. "You
wouldn't believe how many customs officials I had to bribe to
get a case of it." He paused. "I hope you appreciate that."

"I, for one, appreciate the hell out of it," said Kip. He was
about to take another swig when one of the Orange-Eye camp
servants noticed that none of us were using glasses, and immediately brought over one for each of us.

"Thanks," I said, filling my glass and taking a sip. I turned
to Markham and smiled. "I never noticed it before, but somehow it doesn't taste as good this way."

"Wait until we find Michael Drake," said Markham. "Then
you'll be able to fill your swimming pool with the stuff."

"I don't have a pool."

"You will."

"You really think so?" asked Kip. "I mean, it'll make headlines for a week or two, but after that who will give a damn?"

"You have no soul, Mr. Ngami," said Markham. "We're em-
barking on a great adventure here. We're pitting our skills and
courage against everything this world, and possibly other worlds
as well, can throw at us." He paused. "Think about it. We have
the means to literally vaporize Bushveld, but instead we're
armed with weapons that will give animals and enemies a fair
chance to escape or fight back. We are living off the land, as our
ancestors did when they opened up the last unexplored areas of
Earth and Peponi and Faligor."

He took another sip, then turned back to Kip.

"And the stakes aren't just finding a lost man, Mr. Ngami,"
he continued. "We're not after just *any* man. We're after Michael
Drake, the most famous and accomplished medical doctor in

the history of our race. Billions of people will die if we don't find him; hundreds of millions will die if we don't find him soon. The man is a saint. He'd share his research if he knew we needed him, but he's been isolated for more than a decade, working on his own, with no knowledge that the disease has spread to tens of thousands of worlds. Now," he added, staring directly into Kip's eyes, "do you really think that the man who finds him and brings him back to the Democracy will be forgotten in two weeks' time? This is the adventure of the century! Our goal isn't merely to kill some record animal or find and excavate a forgotten city. No, we've got a more vital mission: We're trying to save a sizable portion of the human race, and if we bring Michael Drake back with us, we'll be honest-to-God *heroes*"—he almost struck a heroic pose for an imaginary camera—"since without us he would never know how badly he's needed. I don't know about you, but I've always wanted to be a hero."

Markham looked around the campfire, his eyes mirroring his enthusiasm. "Each of you will be offered enormous sums of money to tell your stories to a literary collaborator. Mr. Kerr will be able to write his own ticket for his next documentary camerawork. Mr. Stone will be given his choice of museums to run. Mr. Arnaz will win a shelf full of awards. And you, Mr. Ngami, will no longer be a simple mechanic who keeps helioplanes and safari vehicles in working order." I could see Kip's eyes brighten, and he looked for all the world like an athlete ready to destroy the opposition after his coach's pregame pep talk. "Oh, no, Mr. Ngami. After you make your millions from your book, on which you will not have to write a single word, you will be offered your choice of corporate directorships. Probably you'll choose half a dozen or so, to assure you continuing prestige and income. Then you might franchise your name on two dozen savage worlds as the one trustworthy and reliable upscale tour guide."

"I could live with that," admitted Kip.

"Somehow I thought you might," said Markham with a smile.

"And what do *you* get out of it?" asked Kip. "More than us, I'll bet."

"It's a story," answered Markham. "I get to be the first to tell it."

"That's all?"

"That's enough." Kip looked dubious, and Markham, noticing it, added, "But there will be more than enough money and glory to go around."

"So do you want the money and glory, or do you want to find Michael Drake?" persisted Kip.

"They're one and the same," answered Markham.

"You think so, do you?"

"Absolutely."

"So what else have you covered before you decided to bring Michael Drake back to civilization?"

"I was there when Nicobar Lane killed the very last Devilowl," he said. "I covered Alpha Triconis going supernova. I was the only journalist present when the priesthood of Einstein III committed mass suicide." He paused and lit a smokeless cigar. "But none of them compared to this."

"You were there when all those thousands of priests set fire to themselves?" I asked.

"Yes. So was Mr. Kerr."

"Hell of a story."

"No more so than the others."

"Surely you can't be comparing the deaths of a quarter million men with one Devilowl!"

"In terms of their value to the galaxy, who's to say which was more important?" responded Markham. "There are still close to a trillion Men; there will never be another Devilowl."

"If you feel that way, why didn't you try to talk Lane out of killing the Devilowl?" asked Kip.

"My job is reporting what happens, not altering it," answered Markham firmly.

"Which makes you a hell of a journalist and not much of a human being," said Kip.

Markham shrugged. "We've had good human beings, and look at the mess they've made of things. It's time we had some good journalists."

"How long have you been at it?" I asked.

A Vermin Zapper glowed as a pair of batlike creatures came too close to it and were instantly vaporized. "Journalism? Ever since I got out of school. I always knew that this was what I wanted to do—to go out to the edge of civilization, to see new worlds and new races, and to have someone pay me for it. If I were less handy with words, I'd probably be doing *your* job, or perhaps Mr. Vaughn's. I just know that I've always wanted to see beyond the next hill, or the next world."

"You could have been a scientist," suggested Kip. "A field man."

"Science bores me," said Markham. "Words and images fascinate me."

"And yet here you are, trying to find the most important scientist of all."

"He's a doctor, not a scientist."

"Since when did medical research cease to be a science?" I asked.

"Touché, Mr. Stone," said Markham. "All right, here I am, trying to find the most important scientist of all."

"You're here because *he's* here," said Kip. "Do you ever feel like a parasite?"

"Never, Mr. Ngami," said Markham, and I could see he was trying to keep his annoyance from becoming anger. "If I weren't here, Michael Drake would never know how bad the situation had become, might never emerge from the jungle to present us with his findings and his theories. The journalists who descend upon him *after* we bring him out are the parasites, making their reputations solely because *our* efforts were successful."

We continued drinking until the bottle was empty, and then Kerr and Arnaz went off to assemble the equipment they would be using the next day. Kip and I stayed by the fire with Markham.

"You know something?" said Kip, who was drunk by now.

"What?" asked Markham.

"You're an interesting guy. I can't figure you out."

"What puzzles you, Mr. Ngami?"

"You've spent most of your career on the Frontier," said Kip. "Are you beating your competitors to stories out here, or are you hiding from the competition?"

"That's an insulting question," said Markham. "I don't propose to answer it."

"Got another one for you," continued Kip. "If you're so goddamned good, how come I never heard of you before?"

"I'm not responsible for your lack of culture," said Markham. He stared irritably into the dark. "Don't those damned Orange-Eyes ever stop singing?"

"I like their singing," said Kip, who seemed determined to have a confrontation with Markham.

Markham turned to me. "I'm trying to be a patient man, but you'd better help Mr. Ngami to his bubble before he says something I can't forgive."

I nodded and got Kip to his feet.

"Come on," I said. "You can lean on me."

He took an unsteady step, then another, and slowly but surely I got him to his bubble, where he collapsed on his bed. I figured my duty was to get him there, and didn't extend to undressing him, so I returned to the campfire.

"He doesn't like me very much," remarked Markham, when I sat down again.

"He hardly knows you," I said, without answering him directly. "That's the liquor talking."

"I doubt it," said Markham thoughtfully. He continued staring at the fire. "Most people don't like me. They never have." He paused for a long moment, watching the flickering of the flames and listening to the sounds of the Bushveld night, and then sighed deeply. "For years I comforted myself with a statement I'd read or heard somewhere—that they didn't have to like me, but they were damned well going to respect me."

I stared at him silently, waiting for him to continue.

"Well, I'm respected, and I'm not liked," he said, staring off into the darkness. "You know what? It was a lousy bargain."

He got up and walked off toward his bubble.

5

We were off early the next morning. The first couple of hours saw us crossing a beautiful green savannah, with enormous herds of herbivores grazing in the distance. A number of animals stopped their grazing to watch us, since they had never seen a vehicle before, and by the same token, since they hadn't been hunted from vehicles, they felt no compulsion to run away.

There was one species in particular, a mottled gold and red hornless browser, perhaps four hundred pounds on the average, that stood out like a sore thumb against the background of scrub and grasses.

"That's curious," remarked Markham, pointing to them.

"What is?"

"Those creatures."

"Mottlebucks," I said. "At least, that's what I named them last time I was here. I don't know if it caught on." I looked across the savannah at them. "What's so curious?"

"They kind of blow a hole in the theory of protective coloration, don't they?" remarked Markham. "You can spot one of them from a mile away." He paused and frowned. "I wonder if there might be a story there—the species that disproves the theory."

"You'd look damned silly after you were proved wrong," I said. "But you might want to do a feature about how even Mottlebucks *support* the theory of protective coloration."

"But they don't," he insisted.

I ordered our Orange-Eye driver to approach the herd slowly. When we were about five hundred yards away we stopped, and I told Markham to look at them through his field glasses.

"Okay, I'm looking," he said.

"What do you see?"

"Mottlebucks."

"Look more closely," I said.

"Son of a bitch!" he said. "About every twelfth one is carrying some major wounds, like a predator clawed at its rump and missed, or fell off." He turned to me. "Is that what I'm supposed to see?"

I nodded. "They stand out from a mile away, like you said. But when they spot a predator and take off as a herd, the mottling confuses the predator. He can spot them from even farther away than you can, but once he's close to a bunch of them in flight he can't differentiate their outlines, so he frequently misses his mark." I pointed to some nearby herbivores, similar in shape, but a shade of muted brown. "You won't see any wounds on these fellows here. When a predator goes after one of them, he makes a kill or else it's a clean miss."

"Now, that's fascinating!" enthused Markham. "You bet your ass there's a story here. Maybe two!"

A moment later he jumped out of the vehicle, momentarily startling the herd, which ran a few hundred yards, then turned and watched him walk to the next vehicle in line, where he gave explicit instructions to Arnaz and Kerr. Soon they, too, were standing on the ground, their holo equipment in hand.

"Okay, let's go," said Markham, returning and climbing back onto his seat.

"What about *them?*" I asked, indicating the cameramen.

"They'll join us in a few hours. I want them to get shots of a predator attacking the Mottlebucks, and it's less likely to happen if we're all here."

"Most of Bushveld's predators are nocturnal, especially out here on the open plain," I noted. "Nothing interesting's going to happen before nightfall."

"Then they'll catch up with us tomorrow morning," he replied in a tone of voice that said the subject was closed.

In truth, it made no difference to me. Even if Drake was on Bushveld, we were surely more than a few days from finding him, and if the cameras were elsewhere, it meant we wouldn't be stopping for the heroic hunter to blow away any more innocent animals that wanted nothing more than to be left alone. It was a situation we could all live with—me, Kip, the Orange-Eyes, and especially the game.

The savannah petered out before noon, and we found ourselves in increasingly hilly country, covered with a variety of thorny shrubs, a few of which were actually poisonous to Man. As the character of the countryside changed, so did the nature of the animals we saw. We came upon some huge, horned, three-ton creatures that seemed totally placid until we pulled a little too close to one and it charged us, veering off at an angle at the very last second.

The bugs started getting thicker and nastier, and we activated some of the zappers, though they didn't do much good. Before long Markham, Kip, and I had activated our electronic protection fields. They were no use against anything large and dangerous, but they kept the bugs at bay. The Orange-Eyes seemed oblivious of the insects, though they swarmed over them as eagerly as they attacked us.

In midafternoon Kenny Vaughn radioed us. He'd found a nice clearing by a stream about three miles from where we where, and had left a dead antelope there to mark the spot and provide food for the party.

"That was stupid!" said Markham, grabbing the speaker from me. "If some predator doesn't run off with it, there'll be a zillion insects on it by the time we get there."

"Explain it to him, Enoch," said Kenny, signing off.

"Listen, you . . . !" began Markham, before he realized that the connection had been severed. He turned to me. "All right—explain *what?*"

"He knows better than to leave his kill on the ground, Mr. Markham," I said. "He'll hang it at least thirty feet up a tree. The insects won't bother anything higher than about fifteen feet. And he won't have it lying on a branch where some tree-climbing predator can reach it. He'll hang it down a few feet from the branch by a rope."

"This is standard operating procedure?" asked Markham, his anger already replaced by his endless curiosity.

"That's right. He'll send one of his Orange-Eyes back in an hour or two to police the area."

Markham frowned. "I don't understand."

"You've got to bleed the corpse before you can eat it, and before the blood can coagulate. If nothing's done about the blood, eventually it'll attract other predators. They won't be able to reach the kill, but we don't want them hanging around while we set up camp. So what happened was this: Kenny had his Orange-Eyes dig a hole right under the antelope's branch. He'll slit its jugular and probably a couple of arteries when he hangs it, and once it's finished bleeding the Orange-Eye he sends back will fill in the hole and start a small fire there to totally eradicate the scent of blood."

"Very practical."

"Kenny knows his stuff."

"No argument," said Markham. He stared at the radio for a long moment. "I wish he wasn't so unpleasant. I'd like to hear some of the stories he could tell."

I had no reply, or none that I cared to make to his face, so I simply declared a ten-minute break to stretch our legs and answer calls of nature. Then I waited for Markham to get out of the vehicle so that I could walk in the other direction.

A moment later Kip and I were standing behind a bush, urinating on the ground and hoping we could finish before the insects discovered us, when Markham's voice came to us in what was almost a stage whisper.

"Can something vaguely catlike, with a dark red skin and claws front and back, maybe five hundred pounds, be anything *but* a predator?"

"You've just described a Redpanther," I answered. "Where is it?"

"About forty feet from me."

"Don't move," I said softly. "That's just about the most dangerous killer on the planet. He can cover forty feet with one jump."

"I'm not moving," said Markham calmly. "I'm observing."

"I'll try to sneak around to the car and get a weapon," I said, finishing and fastening my pants.

"There's no need to. I'm not threatening him. He won't attack."

"I hate to disillusion you," I said, "but they attack because they're hungry, not threatened. And sometimes they attack just for the hell of it."

"Then don't startle him," said Markham. "Damn! I wish Kerr or Arnaz was here. Remind me never to leave them both behind in the future."

"Shut up or you won't *have* a future," I said urgently. "Some-

times the sound of a human voice is enough to precipitate an attack."

"This one seems to have broken off a fang somewhere," observed Markham. "Upper left."

"If you can see that, you're too damned close," I said. "Start
backing away."

"Nonsense."

I decided to shut up, since every time I spoke he answered,
and I wasn't kidding about the sound of a voice. Kip was already on his way to the second vehicle, and he reached it a few
seconds ahead of me.

"You sure you *want* to save him?" he asked as I reached for
the sonic weapon.

"If he dies, who pays our way home?" I countered.

"Then use the Burner," he said, indicating the laser rifle.
"It's surer than the Screecher."

"Yeah, but the Screecher won't put any holes in it, and then
he won't spend the next couple of weeks bitching about how we
ruined his trophy."

"*His?* You make it sound like he's the one who's going to
kill it."

"Five'll get you ten that's the way he's going to tell it," I said,
checking the Screecher's charge and heading off toward
Markham.

I came up behind him about a minute later. He hadn't been
kidding; he was an easy jump away from one of the biggest Redpanthers I had ever seen. The creature saw me, tensed, and
growled deep in its throat. Markham, squatting on his
haunches, didn't move.

"Isn't he beautiful?" whispered Markham.

"And dangerous," I replied.

"God divided the universe into meat-eaters and meat. He
and I are meat-eaters. We understand each other."

"He doesn't understand shit," I said. "He just knows that you're intruding on his territory. I think I'd better shoot him."

"I forbid it, unless he charges me."

The Redpanther's tail twitched nervously, as its eyes seemed to look deep into my soul.

"What do you plan to do?" I asked. "Just keep staring at each other until it's too dark too see?"

"He'll leave soon," said Markham.

"It's what direction he leaves in that worries me."

Markham stood up slowly. The Redpanther growled again, but didn't move.

"You see? I told you he wouldn't charge."

"It'll take us sixty seconds to reach the vehicle," I said. "He can do it in five. You're not safe yet."

He picked up a small rock and, before I could stop him, hurled it in the Redpanther's face. The beast snarled, leaped to its feet, and took off like a bat out of hell. The tall grasses swallowed it up a few seconds later.

"You're not exactly the stuff heroic legends are made of, are you?" said Markham contemptuously as he began walking back to the vehicle.

"You could probably pull that damnfool stunt six times in a row and get away with it," I said. "The seventh Redpanther would rip you to shreds. What's the point of taking unnecessary risks?"

"Who says it was unnecessary?"

"Suppose you tell me why it *wasn't* unnecessary."

"How can I tell my readers what it feels like to stand up to a Redpanther if I don't know?"

"And what if it had been that seventh one?"

"That's why I didn't throw the stone until you were behind me with a weapon."

"I'm not Kenny Vaughn," I pointed out. "I might have missed him."

"I'm not paying you to miss," he said as we finally reached the vehicle and he climbed back in.

How do you answer something like that? It wasn't quite a compliment, and it wasn't quite an insult, and it may even have been a statement of fact as he saw it. At any rate, I replaced the Screecher in its container, climbed into the vehicle, and told the driver to proceed.

We reached the clearing by the river just before twilight. Sure enough, Kenny had hung a large herbivore well above the insects' invisible ceiling, and a small fire was blazing just beneath it. There was, of course, no sign of Kenny and his Orange-Eyes.

"Where is he now?" asked Markham.

I shrugged. "Probably halfway to tomorrow night's camp."

Markham spat in the dirt. "This can't keep up for the whole expedition," he complained.

"I'm sure it won't," I said. "But he's got to blaze a trail until we find one to follow."

That seemed to satisfy him this time, and I gratefully left his presence to supervise the Orange-Eyes setting up the camp. I figured that if Kerr and Arnaz hadn't shown up yet, or even contacted us via the radio, they weren't going to catch up with us until tomorrow, so we didn't erect their bubbles.

Markham wandered by a few minutes later. "You've got four bubbles," he noted.

I explained that I didn't expect the cameramen to show up.

"You've got too many, not too few."

"Well, there's always a chance that Hiram Wentzel has set out after us and will reach camp in the next few hours."

"Forget it."

"It's unlikely," I admitted. "But it's a possibility."

"He's not showing up," said Markham with total assurance. "Take the bubble down."

"How do you know?"

"I radioed Fort Capstick this morning and fired him."

"Who told you you could do that?" I demanded.

"It's my expedition."

"But he came here on *my* word, damn it!"

"He'll be paid for his fuel and time."

"I wish that fucking Redpanther had ripped your head off!" I snapped.

"I'm sure you do," said Markham with no show of emotion.

"What the hell are we going to do when one of us comes down with some jungle fever, or breaks a bone?" I continued, still furious.

"I've sent for another doctor. One who will show up tomorrow, or suffer the same consequences as your Dr. Wentzel," said Markham. He paused. "My publishers demand excellence from me. I demand that same excellence of the people *I* hire."

"His ship had a mechanical problem," I protested. "That's hardly his fault."

"And if Kenny Vaughn's gun has a mechanical problem when he's being charged by a Landwhale or a Redpanther, it'll hardly be *his* fault—but he'll be just as dead."

"What's one got to do with the other?"

"I won't tolerate slovenliness, whatever the cause."

I glared at him in the fading light of Bushveld's sun. "You'd just better be as good a journalist as you're supposed to be," I said at last.

"Better."

6

I was up at sunrise, as usual, and had breakfast organized before Kip and Markham emerged from their bubbles. We'd been contacted by Kerr and Arnaz, who had spent the entire day and night fruitlessly waiting for a kill and wanted further instructions. Markham had made up his mind during his encounter with the Redpanther that he didn't want to be without at least one cameraman, and since Kerr and Arnaz shared a single vehicle, he reluctantly agreed that both of them should rejoin us.

I decided to wait until they caught up with us; it's much easier for two novices to find a camp by a river, with a fire burning and bubbles still up, than to find a pair of vehicles in the middle of a vast uninhabited plateau—our destination for the day—so we lingered by the campfire after breakfast, luxuriating in the warming rays of the sun.

"Damned wag makes a nice cup of coffee," said Markham as

one of the camp boys poured refills for us. "Credit where credit is due."

"Wag?" repeated Kip.

"Right. Wag."

"I've never heard that term before. What does it mean?"

Markham pointed at the Orange-Eyes, who were puttering around the camp area. "Them."

"That can't be a local term," said Kip. "You've never been here before."

"It's not," answered Markham. "I think it originated on Peponi or some other colony world."

"What's its derivation?" asked Kip.

"The colonists had some term for the natives—I don't know what it was—and it was determined by some official with too much time on his hands that it was offensive. So the colonial government decreed that all the natives should be called Worthy Alien Gentlemen." He snorted contemptuously. "That lasted about an afternoon; then everyone started using the acronym instead. It didn't take long to spread all over the Democracy and the Inner Frontier."

"It sounds insulting to me," said Kip.

"Why?" asked Markham. He gestured to a couple of nearby Orange-Eyes. "Do you think *they* care?"

"They might, if they knew what you were saying."

Markham shrugged. "Then don't tell them, and we'll all be happy."

Kip stared at him. He seemed about to reply, but then shrugged and sipped his coffee.

I activated my pocket computer, had it produce a hologram of a map and float it in the air just in front of me. I instructed it to highlight Fort Capstick and show how far we had come. The terrain had been more rugged than I had anticipated, and we hadn't made as much progress as we had planned. I estimated we were still a few days from the last sighting of Michael Drake—if indeed it *was* Michael Drake.

"And of course," I concluded, after explaining the marks on the map, "that was five years ago. Who knows where he is today? He could be halfway around the planet, or even halfway across the galaxy—if he's alive at all."

"Well, if it was easy, the rewards wouldn't be so great," said Markham.

"Do you *ever* get discouraged?" asked Kip.

"If I do, I keep it to myself," answered Markham. "I don't approve of public displays of emotion, and of those emotions that I can't abide, cowardice and self-doubt lead the list."

"Must be nice to always know you're right."

"It's a comfort," agreed Markham with no trace of humor or sarcasm.

"I had my computer pull up one of your books last night," continued Kip.

"Oh? Which one?"

"The one about the discovery of gold on Karimon."

"What did you think of it?"

"You're a brilliant writer, Mr. Markham," said Kip. "I can't take that away from you. You made me feel like I was right there alongside you. I could smell the smells and taste the tastes. You're almost as good as you think you are."

"But you don't like me very much, do you?" asked Markham.

"That's a hell of a thing to ask," protested Kip. "We've got to live in each other's pockets for months, maybe years."

"I know. Answer it anyway."

"No."

"No you won't answer, or no you don't like me?"

"Take your choice," said Kip.

"In that case, we're almost even," said Markham. "I don't

like you either—but unlike you, I have no idea if you're any good at your profession."

"You'll find out soon enough," said Kip.

"I intend to."

Big Shoulders approached just then, and walked up to me.

"Ready break camp?" he asked.

"Soon," I said. "I'll let you know when."

He grunted something and walked away.

" 'Ready break camp?' " repeated Markham mockingly. "You would think the stupid wag would learn to speak Terran properly."

"This is *his* world, and there are only a couple of hundred Men on it," I pointed out. "He probably wonders why we don't speak his language."

"I doubt if he wonders about anything except filling his belly," said Markham contemptuously.

"We'd better hope he does," I replied, "or we could find ourselves sleeping in the rain, shitting on the grass, and eating beetles for breakfast."

Markham chuckled and stared at Big Shoulders as the Orange-Eye returned to his own side of the camp, as if trying to imagine him with a functioning brain. Finally he gave it up and shook his head. "Enough bleeding-heart bullshit. I can do better alone on his world than he could do on any of ours." He got to his feet, dusted himself off, and stalked over to his bubble.

"I wonder if it was something we said?" mused Kip. Suddenly he grinned. "And if we said it again, would he leave again?"

It wasn't worth answering, so I didn't say anything. We sat there sipping our coffee for another hour, and finally the two cameramen pulled up.

"How'd it go?" asked Kip.

"Terrible," replied Kerr. "They were making kills all night.

We could hear them, could almost smell them. But every time we tried to get close, they ran off."

"So we not only didn't get any shots of the Redpanthers *making* their kills," added Arnaz, "we couldn't even get shots of them *eating* their goddamned kills."

"But *we* sure got eaten," said Kerr. "Where's the med kit? I must have five hundred insect bites."

As he spoke, he drew near enough so that I could see his right eye, which was almost swollen shut, and his neck, which was covered with reddish spots. I yelled to Big Shoulders to bring the kit, and a moment later the two cameramen had smeared healing cream all over themselves.

"I take it the doctor hasn't arrived yet," said Arnaz.

"He's been fired," I said. "We're expecting a different one later today."

"Where's the boss?" asked Kerr, as Big Shoulders carried the med kit back to the vehicle.

"He got pissed at me," said Kip, "so he's in his bubble, probably planning on the most embarrassing way to sack me."

"You don't know him at all," said Kerr. "If he's in his bubble, he's working on a story. He probably hasn't given you two seconds' worth of thought."

"I'd sure be thinking of dumping *him* if things were reversed. He's a strange Man."

"What other kind of Man would be leading an expedition like this, to find someone he's never met before, someone who's been missing and presumed dead for more than a decade?" replied Kerr with a smile. "Of *course* he's a strange Man." He paused. "I'll tell you something else about him. When he comes out of his bubble, there won't be a word about whatever argument you had that sent him there."

"Are you saying he doesn't hold grudges, either?" said Kip disbelievingly.

"No, he holds 'em longer than most Men—but he doesn't let them interfere with business."

"Maybe he should have been a politician," suggested Kip.

"He could have been," responded Kerr. "But he likes what he does better."

Suddenly I heard a crash, and then Markham was bellowing inside his bubble. Next came a *crack!*, and a few seconds later Cotton Jacket came racing out of the bubble, a thin line of blood staining the back of his ancient coat.

"What the hell's going on?" I demanded.

"I drop tray."

"What did Markham do to you?"

"My fault," he said. "Tomorrow I do right."

"Did he whip you?" I persisted.

"I drop tray."

"I don't care what you did!" I snapped. "I want to know what *he* did to you!"

"Tomorrow no drop tray," he promised, walking off toward the area where the Orange-Eyes were clustered.

"Does he make a habit of beating the hired help?" I demanded of the cameramen.

"Leave it be," said Kerr. "Cotton Jacket doesn't mind it, so why should you?"

"Because I'm the leader of this expedition, that's why!" I said heatedly.

"You are, huh? Then what's Markham?"

"He's a client."

Kerr snorted derisively. "Without you, we still have an expedition," he pointed out. "Without him we don't. You might think about that."

"He can't go around beating the Orange-Eyes whenever they make a mistake."

"Sure he can," said Kerr. "He's the boss. Besides, the

Orange-Eyes don't seem to mind. You didn't see Cotton Jacket protesting, did you?"

"He doesn't know he has the right to protest."

"Then go tell him, and I'll bet you a week's pay he still doesn't protest."

I glared at him for a long moment. "Nevertheless, I've got to have this out with Markham. It can't happen again."

Almost as if on cue, Markham emerged from his bubble.

"I see you found us," he said to Kerr and Arnaz. "Ready to go?"

"As soon as we have some coffee and take a shower," said Kerr.

"Have one of the wags bring some food along. You can eat while we're traveling."

"Come on, Mr. Markham," complained Arnaz. "We've been up for twenty-six hours. We've been driving for most of the morning, and we haven't eaten or had a chance to relax. Michael Drake'll keep for another few hours."

Markham turned to him. "You can join us or stay behind, as you wish. But I'm taking all three vehicles, and we're not coming back until we find Michael Drake, or prove to my satisfaction that he's not on Bushveld. The choice is yours."

"Some choice," muttered Arnaz.

"We've been through this on other expeditions, Mr. Arnaz," said Markham. "I will not accommodate malingerers."

"Malingerers?" repeated Arnaz angrily. "Next time you want something extra from me, I'm charging overtime."

"Your contract specified that you were being paid one fee for the entire expedition, not by the week or the hour," noted Markham. "And it was with my publishers, not with me. So if you're unhappy, take it up with them when we get back. But right now you have a decision to make. We're breaking camp and pulling out in twenty minutes. Are you coming along?"

"Of course I'm coming along, you son of a bitch."

Markham smiled. "That's more like the Arnaz I know."

"Fuck you."

"I like spirit in a man." Suddenly Markham's smile vanished. "Just don't overdo it." He turned to me. "Tell the wags to get off their butts and go to work."

"In a minute," I said. "We have to talk first."

"Okay," he said. "Talk."

"In private."

"Come into my bubble."

I followed him, waited for him to sit down in a camp chair, and then seated myself opposite him.

"You beat Cotton Jacket a few minutes ago."

"That's right. He spilled a pitcher of coffee."

"On my safaris, we don't whip our servants."

"On mine we do," he said. "And as long as I'm paying the bills, this is mine."

"Spilling coffee is not a whipping offense anywhere in the galaxy."

"It is now," said Markham. "This isn't my first safari. I've dealt with ignorant wags before. If you want to make an impression on them, you don't politely chastise them. You beat the shit out of them and then they remember."

"These Orange-Eyes were supplied by Kenny Vaughn. If he finds out you whipped one of them . . ."

"Your friend Mr. Vaughn should have supplied us with better-trained wags," said Markham with no show of fear at what Kenny might do. "They'll be more careful workers when I return them than they were when I got them."

"If they live that long."

"I didn't put Cotton Jacket in the hospital," replied Markham. "I just taught him an object lesson that he's not likely to forget right away. Why don't you ask Big Shoulders if I was right or wrong?"

I glared at him, but deep in my heart, I knew that Big Shoulders would agree with him. In fact, I'd seen the Orange-Eye kicking a couple of his workers when he thought they were loafing.

There were rules that governed every civilized world—but Bushveld *wasn't* a civilized world, and I suddenly realized that, possibly excepting Kip, I was the only Man on the planet who would give two seconds' thought to an Orange-Eye who'd been physically disciplined by a Man.

If even Cotton Jacket didn't care, why should I?

But I did.

7

I got up, sought out Big Shoulders, and told him to break down the camp. Within fifteen minutes we were packed and ready to leave. I tried to raise Kenny on the radio to tell him we were on our way, but I couldn't get through to him—probably he had deactivated his set—so we just took off toward the long plateau and assumed we'd be able to contact him later.

As we rose about half a mile in altitude, the air became cooler and drier, and suddenly we started passing huge herds of game again, though of a different type than we had seen the previous day. There were perhaps a dozen species of herbivore, plus seemingly endless numbers of Landwhales. We were even fortunate enough—I use the word "fortunate" advisedly, as it was a horrible and bloody sight—to get some footage of a pack of spotted Killerdogs separating a newborn Landwhale from its mother and bringing it down, only to be run off by half a dozen huge Landwhale males before they could consume their hard-won meal. After a few minutes the Landwhales left the corpse, and a Redpanther, turning scavenger for the day, stole the kill and carried it off.

After another ten or twelve miles, we came to the first native village we had seen since leaving Fort Capstick. It looked pretty much like the ones I had seen on my last trip to Bushveld: perhaps forty square huts—some large, some small, but all square—with walls made of mud and dried dung, roofs an assortment of woven reeds, all of them set up in some kind of strange geometric design that seemed never to vary from one village to the next.

"Big Shoulders!" I shouted, as our vehicles came to a stop.

The Orange-Eye left his own vehicle and walked up to stand just outside my door.

"The village looks empty," I said. "Where are all the people?"

"In their huts," he said. "They wait see if you are friendly."

"Go tell them we mean them no harm, that we wish to be friends. Explain to them that we are seeking Michael Drake, and ask if they know where he is."

He grunted an acknowledgment and walked into the middle of the village—and one by one, the male Orange-Eyes, most of them threatening Big Shoulders with their spears, began emerging from their huts.

"I think they're going to kill him," remarked Markham dispassionately.

"If they wanted to kill him, he'd be dead already," I said. "They just want to convince him—and us—that we can't kill *them*."

Big Shoulders said something, one of the Orange-Eyes replied, they spoke rapidly for a few minutes, and finally Big Shoulders turned to the vehicle and gestured for us to come over and join him.

Markham was out of his seat and walking rapidly toward

them before I even began to climb down. He was a lot of things good and bad, but frightened wasn't one of them.

"Doctor Man came, went," said Big Shoulders when we had joined him.

"How do you know it was a doctor?" I asked.

"Babies sick. Doctor Man stabs with metal thorn. Babies all better. Doctor Man spends night, takes food, goes away. Never comes back."

"Sounds like our man, all right," said Kip.

"Ask him how long ago this happened," said Markham.

Big Shoulders said something. The Orange-Eyes looked puzzled. Big Shoulders spoke again. This time one of the Orange-Eyes answered him. Big Shoulders questioned him further, listened, nodded, and turned to us.

"Cannot answer. Long time ago."

"Ask him how many long rains have come and gone," I suggested.

"They do not know," said Big Shoulders. "If they know, they answer."

"Ask anyway."

He asked, and the response was negative. They simply didn't keep track of the years or the rains.

"Well, that's that," I said, turning to Markham. "It could have been five years, it could have been fifteen. And either way, it might not have been Michael Drake."

"It was Drake, all right," said Markham.

"Maybe it was and maybe it wasn't," I said. "But I don't see how you're going to find out from these people."

Markham turned to me. "You're a fool," he said. "Big Shoulders!"

"What?" asked the Orange-Eye.

"How many years does it take an Orange-Eye to grow as tall as you?"

Big Shoulders thought for a moment. "Maybe seventeen,

maybe nineteen." He paused thoughtfully. "I am very tall. Maybe twenty. And many never grow this tall."

"Ask these people to show us some of the children that the doctor saved."

"Of course!" I said. "And if they're not full-grown . . ."

"I suggest in the future you stick to running the expedition and leave the interrogating to me," said Markham.

"I'm sorry," I said defensively. "I didn't think of—"

"I don't give a shit if you're sorry or not!" snapped Markham. "What you did was prove that I can't send you out as a surrogate. I'm going to have to question every fucking tribe of savages myself."

I was about to answer him when an old female brought two young Orange-Eye children up to us.

"These two were saved by the doctor?" asked Markham.

Big Shoulders translated the question. The answer was immediate.

"Yes."

"How old can they be, Big Shoulders?" asked Markham.

"Maybe six, maybe five," opined our Orange-Eye.

"So they were inoculated or otherwise treated no more than five years ago," concluded Markham. "Lane was right. I knew it!"

"All you know is a human doctor was here."

"I checked the immigration records while I was with the governor back at Fort Capstick," said Markham. "Drake is the only human doctor ever to set foot on Bushveld, other than the medics who are assigned to the colonial government, such as it is—and they never leave Fort Capstick." He paused. "This is a Frontier world. Until it's officially incorporated into the Democracy, it may even be illegal for a government employee to medicate the Orange-Eyes."

The children were ushered back to a hut.

"Thank them for me," said Markham.

Big Shoulders swayed uneasily, as if he didn't know quite what to do or say.

"What's the problem?" demanded Markham.

"The Orange-Eyes have done you a favor," I said. "Now they expect a favor in return."

"You mean payment?"

"That's right."

"What the hell do they use for money?" asked Markham.

"They don't use money. They're subsistence farmers. I think they'd be happy for a few pounds of salt." I turned to Big Shoulders. "Is that right?"

"Salt good."

"Then give them their salt and let's be on our way," said Markham, starting to walk back to the vehicle.

"They'll want to thank you," I said.

"It's not necessary."

"If you ever pass this way again and want anything from them, it *is* necessary."

Markham turned and rejoined us.

A moment later Big Shoulders presented the headman of the village with a bag of salt. The headman opened the bag, licked his finger, inserted it, then brought it to his mouth. He closed his eyes and concentrated on the taste, then smiled. Suddenly everyone else was smiling, and then they bowed toward us, and we bowed toward them, and they clapped their hands and we clapped our hands, and finally it was done and we were able to return to the vehicles without offending them.

"Well, Mr. Stone," said Markham, "do you finally believe that Nicobar Lane was right?"

"Probably."

"You're a hard man to convince."

"You don't have to convince me, Mr. Markham," I said. "I signed on for the duration, remember?"

That seemed to satisfy him, and he remained satisfied until

lunchtime, when he remembered that our new doctor was supposed to have joined us.

"Where the hell can he be?" mused Markham.

"It took *us* a couple of days to get here; there's no way he can
make it here from Fort Capstick in one morning."

"He won't be driving. I told him to fly."

"There's no place to land," said Kip. "The terrain's too rough
for anything more than my little fold-up plane."

"Then he'll jump."

"With a parachute?"

"With, without, that's up to him," said Markham. "But if he
wants the job, he'd better catch up with us before sunset."

"*Does* he want the job?" I asked.

"I don't follow you."

"If he's the only doctor on Bushveld, and the government
hired him to work in Fort Capstick, why does he want to leave?
And more to the point, is he even allowed to accept the job?"

"Okay, now I understand," said Markham. "I'm not hiring
the government's doctor. I found out via the radio that the doctor is being visited by a retired relative—an uncle, I think—
who's also a medic. In fact, the man was posted here a few years
ago, before he got the bright idea of recommending his nephew
so he could escape from this dirtball." Suddenly Markham
grinned. "When he heard my offer, it took him about three seconds to un-retire." And sure enough, about half an hour later a
small airplane appeared overhead, then buzzed us.

"That looks like our doctor," I said.

"Look at him," said Kip. "He looks like he's going to land.
You don't think he's dumb enough to try it on *this* terrain,
do you?"

I watched the plane as it eased down on the long grass. For
a minute I thought it had made it safely, but then it hit a hidden
boulder, spun crazily, and almost fell over on its side.

A very shaken medic emerged a moment later, followed by

the pilot. Markham greeted them perfunctorily, then had me order Big Shoulders to load the doctor's luggage onto the third vehicle.

Kip and the pilot briefly examined the plane, then returned to us.

"The whole landing gear's busted," said Kip. "So is one of the wings. No way it can take off in its current condition."

"Let the pilot use our radio to call Fort Capstick and tell them his problem," said Markham.

"I appreciate that, sir," said the pilot. "It shouldn't take more than a couple of days to get the parts shipped in from Mayfair II."

"We'll leave you a two-day supply of food," said Markham. He turned to me. "Tell Big Shoulders to see to it."

"I could use some weapons, too. This place is crawling with predators."

"Can't spare any," said Markham.

"Then can you stick around until my parts arrive?" persisted the pilot. "It'll only be two days, three at the most."

"Sorry," said Markham. "We struck Michael Drake's trail this morning. We can't stop now."

"Michael Drake?" repeated the pilot, looking his surprise. "He's been dead for fifteen years."

"Nonsense. He was in a village eight miles from here not five years ago."

"Five years? You call that a hot trail?"

"It's ten years hotter than anything we had prior to this morning," answered Markham.

"But I *can't* stay here alone!" protested the pilot. "The cockpit of that plane is no protection against what's wandering around this place."

"You can stay, or you can come with us, and we'll drop you off at the first friendly village we come to," said Markham. "There's no third way."

"You've got me over a barrel, you bastard," said the pilot bitterly. "I'll come along."

"All right. Grab your gear and ride in the second truck."

As the pilot returned to the plane, Markham called back to Arnaz and Kerr. "Did you get the landing?"

"Yes," came the answer.

"Pity we can't get some footage of some Hooktooths or Redpanthers trying to dig him out of the cockpit," sighed Markham, "but I suppose one can't have everything."

"You could make him go back to the cockpit and hope they come by," suggested Kip sardonically.

When I saw the expression on Markham's face—the man was actually considering it—I could have kicked Kip.

Finally Markham shrugged. "No," he said. "It could take a couple of days before they spot him. We can't afford the time." He turned to Kip. "I'm glad to see you're finally starting to use your brain, Mr. Ngami. There's hope for you after all."

Kip was so surprised he just shook his head as if to clear it, and spent the afternoon riding in stunned silence.

8

The pilot's name was Stuart. I never found out if it was his first name or his last. He didn't talk much, just glared a lot at the back of Markham's neck. If Markham was aware of it, he didn't show it.

The doctor, whose name was Satschwechewani Rashid, rode up front with us in the first vehicle. He didn't like being called "Doc" or "Sawbones," so he settled for Rashid after it became obvious that no one was going to pronounce his first name to his satisfaction.

"How long were you on Bushveld?" I asked.

"Just under a year," he replied.

"Why so short a time?"

"I was a doctor—a damned good one. But there can't be three hundred Men on this whole planet, then or now. If that's your entire patient base, and you're good at your job, you can go weeks without having to treat anyone. I didn't spend all those years studying so I could vegetate on Bushveld."

"How about the Orange-Eyes?" I asked.

"I give up," he said. "How *about* the Orange-Eyes?"

"I mean, why didn't you treat them too?"

"Against regulations," replied Rashid. "Besides, they may look a bit like us, but they have totally different metabolisms and nervous and circulatory systems. An injection that could immunize you against one of the diseases that's endemic on this world might very well send an Orange-Eye into shock, or kill him. To the best of my knowledge, there are no textbooks on their physiology."

"Maybe you should write one," said Kip seriously.

"It would take me twenty years or more to do it properly," answered Rashid. "And except for a few libraries where it would sit and never be accessed, do you know how many copies I could sell? One to each doctor who set up shop on Bushveld and wanted to treat Orange-Eyes." He smiled sardonically. "Why, in the next thousand years, my estate might sell as many as, oh, I don't know, four or five copies right here on the planet. Besides," he concluded, "I'm retired."

"Not anymore," I pointed out.

"Touché," he said wryly. "If it'll make you feel any better, sooner or later someone is going to write that book. We control the galaxy, after all, and knowledge is power. We have to know all we can about every race we plan to dominate. But the Orange-Eyes are still living in huts, and they still have a barter economy. They have nothing we want. Once they do—or once they're so militarily powerful that we can't ignore them—that's when the book will be written."

"So until then they remain ignorant of hygiene and die of every disease that comes along?" asked Kip.

"Except for ybonia, there's never been a cross-species disease," replied Rashid. "Which is to say that whatever ails them was ailing them long before Man showed up. There's no need for any of us to feel any guilt about it."

"So we don't feel guilty about infecting them," persisted Kip. "Does that mean we should feel equally innocent when we might have the wherewithal to cure them and we choose to ignore them instead?"

"We may be the banker and the policeman to the galaxy," answered Rashid, "but we're not ready to be the doctor to it as well." He paused. "Right now almost every human medical researcher is working full-time on a cure for ybonia. Our first obligation is to save our own race; once that's done we'll worry about the others."

"Makes sense to me," said Markham from his position at the vehicle's controls. I hadn't even thought he was listening. "Still, once we accomplish our mission, we'll free millions of doctors up for other things."

"What *is* your mission?" asked Rashid.

"We have come to Bushveld to find Michael Drake and bring him back to the Democracy, hopefully with the cure for ybonia," replied Markham.

"You're kidding, right?"

"Why should you think so?" asked Markham.

"Michael Drake's been dead for the past dozen years or so," said Rashid.

"He was within a few yards of where we are right now no more than five years ago."

"You have proof of that?"

"Perhaps not enough to satisfy a court, but more than enough for me, yes," replied Markham.

"Amazing!" said Rashid. "Michael Drake! I'd give my right arm to meet him."

"Stick around and perhaps you will," said Markham confidently.

We drove on for another few miles, and then, suddenly, we heard a crash and a lot of shouting. We jumped down to the ground as our vehicle stopped, and saw that the third vehicle had hit a huge rock and turned over onto its side. The driver, whose name was Crooked Leg, had been thrown into the tall grass at roadside; he was writhing and moaning, but still alive.

Kip and I raced up to the vehicle and began examining the engine while Rashid gave Crooked Leg water and tried to make him comfortable. Finally Kip looked up at me.

"If I had the spare parts I needed, and a garage, and a power source, I *might* be able to get it running again." He sighed. "But out here, under these conditions . . ." He froze, and his eyes widened. "Son of a bitch!" He raced around to the back of the truck. *"Goddammit!"* he bellowed.

"What is it?" I asked, joining him.

"Take a look," he said, pointing to the airplane's crushed wing. "Isn't that just wonderful?"

"What the hell happened?" asked Markham, walking up to us.

"The vehicle hit a rock," I said.

"Damage report?"

"It's dead," said Kip. "So's the plane."

The skin on Markham's face seemed to tighten. He became totally expressionless, but just the same I found it frightening.

"This rock," he said. "It was on the same road that all three vehicles were on, right?"

"Yes, sir," said Kip, still furious over the loss of his plane.

"And the first two drivers missed it, right?"

"Right."

"Bring me the driver who hit it."

"I don't know if he's capable of standing up," I said.

"He won't have to stand for long."

Kip, who was every bit as mad at Crooked Leg as Markham was, walked over to him without a word and lifted him to his feet. He was bleeding from half a dozen major cuts and abrasions, but he was awake and alert.

Markham stared at the driver for a moment, then walked to

the first vehicle, rummaged through it, and returned with the whip he had used on Cotton Jacket.

"I told you," I said. "We don't whip Orange-Eyes."

"I know what you told me," he said softly. "Call Big Shoulders over here."

I did as he asked, wondering what he had in mind.

"Big Shoulders," he said when the headman arrived, "this careless Orange-Eye has killed a vehicle. He struck a rock that the other drivers avoided. Because of this, your people will now have to carry on their backs everything that was loaded onto the vehicle. We have no choice about this; we must have our supplies, and we cannot bring the vehicle back to life. Do you understand?"

"Understand," said Big Shoulders.

"Crooked Leg is the Orange-Eye who is responsible," he said, indicating the wounded driver. "What do you think his punishment should be?"

"Kill him," said Big Shoulders instantly.

A tiny smile passed across Markham's face. "Mr. Stone doesn't approve of killing."

"He is wrong."

"You know it and I know it, but this one time we shall honor Mr. Stone's wishes." He handed the whip to Big Shoulders. "Here. Punish him, but do not kill him."

Big Shoulders took the whip, and directed some of his people to pull the driver to a secluded patch of grass behind some nearby trees.

"I trust you're satisfied, Mr. Stone," said Markham. "I am not administering any punishment whatsoever."

"Killing's too good for that fucking Orange-Eye!" muttered Kip, still examining the shattered wing of his plane.

Rashid walked up to me. "Are you really going to be a party to this?" he demanded.

"No Man is," said Markham. He stared coldly at the medic.

"And no Man is going to stop it, either." He turned to me. "You look unhappy, Mr. Stone."

"You know why."

"Crooked Leg is being paid ten credits a month. That vehicle he destroyed has a market value of fifty-eight thousand credits. He has a projected working life of thirty years. The market places the value of the vehicle at more than fifteen times the value of his entire working life. For the length of this expedition, it may well be worth sixty times that much. He—and the rest of these wags—is going to learn a very painful object lesson."

"There are better ways."

"I've never found one," said Markham. "And neither has your friend Big Shoulders."

And then we heard the sounds of the whip, and Crooked Leg's screams. The whip came down again and again, its *hisscrack!* the only sound to break the silence of the morning. Finally it stopped.

Big Shoulders had his Orange-Eyes drag Crooked Leg back, then laid him down on the ground at roadside. Rashid came over and knelt down next to him, examining the wounds.

"Those are ugly lacerations," he said grimly.

"Can you do something for him?" I asked.

"I don't know," answered Rashid, his voice echoing his frustration. "The antibiotic salve I would use on you might be toxic to an Orange-Eye."

"Can't you try?"

He shook his head. "I'll clean the wounds as best I can without causing him too much pain, but I can't in good conscience give him any human medication." He shrugged helplessly. "I simply don't know enough about the Orange-Eye metabolism."

"All right," I said, exhaling heavily. "Do whatever you can do." I turned to Big Shoulders. "Move whatever will fit into the first two vehicles. Leave a little room in the second vehicle for Crooked Leg."

"He can walk," said Big Shoulders.

"He can barely stand up. Do what I told you."

He grunted an affirmative and headed off.

"Not smart," said Kip.

"I know. You want him dead for busting your plane."

"You stay out here any length of time and you start realizing that maybe Markham's got a point," said Kip. "And if he finds out you're letting that Orange-Eye ride in the back, he'll whip you just as fast as he whipped him."

I looked at Kip, and suddenly I didn't know him anymore.

Finally I walked over to Kerr and Arnaz, who had kept their distance throughout the whipping. "You've seen that before, haven't you?" I asked.

"Every now and then," acknowledged Kerr.

"And you never tried to stop it?"

"He's the boss," responded the cameraman. "And besides, the Orange-Eye had it coming. Everyone else missed the rock. He didn't, and as a result we lost a vehicle and a plane. What kind of punishment do *you* think he deserved?"

"I don't know, but I had hoped we'd outgrown whipping millennia ago."

"Maybe primitive peoples demand primitive approaches," suggested Kerr.

"Do you really believe that?" I challenged him.

"I might as well, because that's what's going to happen, and if I didn't believe it, I'd have an even harder time looking at myself in the mirror each morning."

"That's your only answer?" I demanded.

"I have one," said Arnaz.

"I'm listening."

"I think if you had offered to pay for the vehicle and arranged to have a replacement shipped to us right here—wherever *here* happens to be—he would have been happy not to whip the Orange-Eye. And you know what?"

"What?"

"He'd have been wrong," said Arnaz. "Because without that whipping, the next Orange-Eye driver wouldn't pay any more attention to the road than this one did, and we'd be right back where we started, except that you'd be out about sixty thousand credits."

"Boy, he's really gotten to you two, hasn't he?" I said disgustedly.

"We've been out with him before, and lived to tell about it," responded Kerr. "You may be a nicer guy, but nice isn't a survival trait. If you had your way, it's entirely possible that none of us would live to tell about it."

"Rubbish!" I snapped.

"Yeah?" said Kerr. "I've never asked before, but suppose you tell us exactly how you lost your leg."

"I don't care to discuss it," I said uneasily.

"Somehow I'm not surprised. Well, if you ever do feel like discussing it, I'm ready to listen."

I turned and walked away from them, trying to clear my head. They made so much sense and had all the answers, but when all was said and done, we were less than a week out of Fort Capstick and we'd already fired a doctor, lost a vehicle, and administered a brutal beating to one of the Orange-Eyes who far outnumbered the humans in our party.

Not an auspicious beginning.

9

From that point on, it seemed like the expedition was cursed.

An hour later it began pouring, two months before the long rains were due, and it didn't stop. Our speed, which wasn't much to begin with, slowed to a crawl, as the overloaded vehicles kept getting bogged down in the mud.

When that happened, we all—Men and Orange-Eyes alike—put our shoulders to the vehicles and pushed. At one point we heard a sudden scream of pain. It turned out that Stuart, the pilot, had slipped in the mud just as we got the vehicle moving, and before anyone could stop it again, it had rolled over his right leg, crushing it.

"How is he?" asked Markham, coming over after Rashid had spent a few minutes examining the pilot under the inadequate protection of a nearby tree.

"Not good" was the answer. "Compound fractures above and below the knee. Bone splinters everywhere."

"How soon before he's mobile?"

"That depends how soon we can get him back to the infirmary at Fort Capstick. It's not much of a medical facility," he added apologetically, "but it's all we've got on this planet, and it's equipped to handle something like this."

"I have no idea when we can return him to Fort Capstick. Splint him up and we'll have one of the wags make him a pair of crutches."

"It's not that easy, Mr. Markham," said Rashid.

"Oh? Why not?"

"I just explained: He has multiple compound fractures. His leg is shattered. I can't begin to set it without the proper medical facilities."

"Keep him sedated and do whatever you have to do," said Markham. "We'll dump him at the first village, as planned, and put in a call to Fort Capstick."

"No one's going to fly out in this weather," said Kip.

"Why the hell not?"

"A small plane can't operate in this weather, and the ground's so soft that a big one would sink into it up to its wings if it tried to land."

"I'm sick and tired of getting nothing but negative answers," announced Markham. "Dr. Rashid, he's your patient. Make him as comfortable as you can. Mr. Stone, find us a goddamned village to leave him at, and when we get there put in a call to Fort Capstick."

"The Orange-Eyes won't know how to care for him," protested Rashid, which saved me the trouble of explaining that it could be days before we came to a village at this speed. "He could develop gangrene, or . . ."

"He's not part of this expedition," interrupted Markham. "I agreed to take him along, and I'm willing to let you use our medical supplies on him, but he is not our responsibility."

"He's a Man and he's hurt," shot back Rashid. "That *makes* him our responsibility."

"You're a doctor. Make him stop hurting. That's your only concern. Now do it and stop complaining."

Rashid seemed about to say something, swallowed it, and concentrated on the problem at hand.

"All right," he said. "We'll need to make a litter to move him, and he'll have to ride on the back of one of the vehicles, and we'll have to see to it that he's not constantly exposed to the rain."

"Mr. Stone, take care of it," said Markham, heading back to the protection of the vehicle's cab.

I told Big Shoulders what was needed, and he got four of the Orange-Eyes to work on a litter while two more rigged a canvas screen at the back of the second vehicle.

"What do we do with Crooked Leg?" asked Rashid. "There's not room for both of them to lie down there, not with all the extra cargo we had to put there when the third vehicle died."

"Then he walks," I said.

"He can't!" protested the medic.

"Look," I explained, "one of them has a broken leg and one doesn't. It's an easy call."

"He just took a beating that would put *you* in a hospital for a week! You can't make him walk!"

I looked at Markham, who was sitting in his vehicle, and then back to where Crooked Leg was lying.

"All right," I said. "I've got a feeling that except for Big Shoulders, Markham probably can't tell one Orange-Eye from the other. Shift some of the cargo to my vehicle, then prop Crooked Leg up so he's sitting next to Stuart. If Markham asks who he is and what he's doing, you tell him you recruited one of the Orange-Eyes as a nurse to keep an eye on Stuart."

"He'll want to know why I'm not doing it myself."

"It's dull, boring work, and you're needed to help push the vehicles when they get stuck."

"It's my specialty, and the smallest Orange-Eye is bigger and stronger than me."

"You've got a bad back and can't sit for long periods on this excuse for a road," I said irritably. "You're allergic to water. You broke your toe. Damn it, you're the fucking doctor—*you* think of something!"

"Don't get mad at *me!*" he shot back. "I'm not the cause of this!"

"I know. But it's not beyond him to leave you, Stuart, *and* Crooked Leg behind if he thinks you're disobeying him or slowing him down." I spat into the rain. "It's crazy! Michael Drake passed by here five years ago and he's afraid of being held up for a few hours!"

"Why don't we just strike?" suggested Rashid. "You know—refuse to obey him?"

"A lot of reasons," I said. "Most of them legal. But the main reason is simple enough to understand: I wouldn't put it past him to leave us stranded here with no food and no weapons."

Rashid considered what I had said for a long moment. "Michael Drake had better be alive, and he'd better have found a cure for ybonia."

He walked off to move Crooked Leg, and, tired of being rained on, I reluctantly rejoined Markham in the cab of our vehicle.

"How soon can we start driving again?" were his words of greeting.

"Five minutes, maybe ten," I replied. "And I would hardly call it driving. It's more like sliding."

He stared out the window at the torrential downpour for a

long moment, then spoke again. "I think you'd better try to raise Fort Capstick on the radio."

"Right," I said. "They should know about Stuart."

"Stuart hell. I want to know the weather forecast for the next five days."

"I don't need to talk to Fort Capstick for that," I said. "You'll get a three-hour downpour every day for the next forty days." I forced a smile. "Just like Noah."

"What makes you so sure?"

"Because these are the long rains," I said. "They're early, but if it was just an aberration, it would have stopped by now. The first couple of days you get nonstop rain, and then you get an afternoon monsoon every day for the next six weeks."

"Call them anyway, just to be sure."

"Shall I mention Stuart?"

"*After* you get the forecast."

Kip climbed into the vehicle, crawled onto the boxes that covered his seat, and began drying himself off with a rag he'd left behind.

"Okay, we're ready to move out."

Markham activated the engine and we proceeded at a snail's pace. "Well, the pilot may get wet," he remarked, "but at least his leg isn't going to get jostled. Not at this speed."

"I'm sure he'll take great comfort in that," said Kip sardonically.

"I suppose you're going to say it was my fault he broke his leg," said Markham.

"No, I wasn't."

"He had the chance to stay with his plane. He chose to come with us."

"I know."

"He made a stupid choice," said Markham. "I told him so at the time."

"Did you?" said Kip. "I must have missed it."

"Probably you did," agreed Markham, peering through the window at the nonexistent track he had been following. "Damn! Everything's under water. Which way do I go?"

"Use your compass and keep heading to the west," I said.

"Why west?"

"Because Kenny Vaughn told me he was heading due west," I answered. "We may even overtake him. His vehicle broke down, he's on foot, and he can't be making much progress."

"I think he'd better join us. We can't afford to get separated in weather like this."

"You might want to think very carefully about that," I suggested.

"Why?"

"Because these are Kenny's Orange-Eyes. He's the one who taught Big Shoulders and Cotton Jacket to speak Terran, and you whipped Cotton Jacket yourself and then permitted Big Shoulders to administer a beating to Crooked Leg with your own whip."

"For a major infraction that cost us a vehicle and a plane," Markham pointed out. "Once it's explained to him, I'm sure Mr. Vaughn will understand."

I hoped to hell that Kenny wouldn't understand, because I wanted to continue liking him, but I made no reply.

"In fact," said Markham after further thought, "I want you to contact Mr. Vaughn right now, even before you contact Fort Capstick. Find out where he is, give him our coordinates, and arrange a meeting place for this evening."

"All right," I said. "But I'll have to call from the next vehicle."

"Why?"

"I've forgotten his frequency," I lied. "The other radio is set to it."

Markham came to a stop while I climbed out and ran back

to the cab of the second vehicle. Rashid, who had been foot-slogging alongside Kerr and Arnaz, saw me and quickly joined me.

"Go outside," I told Big Shoulders, who had been driving. "I'll take over."

The Orange-Eye left without a word.

"How is he?" I asked.

"I've got him pretty well sedated," answered Rashid. "But I don't like the look of that leg. If I can't get him to a hospital before gangrene sets in, we may wind up amputating." He looked out the window and added grimly: "I just hope I don't have to do it in the field, with no anesthetic."

"And Crooked Leg?"

"Better than I expected. It's amazing, the punishment these Orange-Eyes can take. By tomorrow he'll probably be strong enough to walk alongside the vehicle."

"Good," I said. "Because we're going to have dinner with his patron saint tonight, and I don't want him in such bad condition that Vaughn feels the need to administer the same kind of punishment to Markham."

"Patron saint?" repeated Rashid. "I don't understand."

"Kenny Vaughn is our meat hunter. He's the man who supplied us with our team of Orange-Eyes. He already dislikes Markham so much that he won't stay in our camp. I don't want to add any fuel to the fire."

"Why not? The bastard deserves it."

"First, because we're stuck with him. And second, because some of us may want to work again sometime."

"I don't understand."

"Markham is sending two stories a day to his ship, which is transmitting to them to his publishers' news syndicate back in the Democracy. Do you really want the reading public of fifty thousand worlds to think you're a coward and a liar and a saboteur—or, in your particular case, a clumsy, drunken butcher—

without being able to say a word in your own defense, without even knowing until you emerge from the bush in a month or a year that you have no reputation left?"

"I see," said Rashid.

"Anyway, that's why I'm contacting Kenny Vaughn on *this* radio," I continued. "So I can speak to him without being overheard."

It took me about five minutes to make contact with Kenny, and his picture kept breaking up, so I finally settled for a straight audio transmission.

"How do you like our weather?" he asked.

"Too dry for my taste," I said, and he laughed. "Where are you?"

"Holed up in a cave," he said. "Had to chase a couple of Horntooths out."

I gave him our coordinates. "How far apart are we?"

"Maybe four or five miles."

"We've had our share of problems," I said. "One of the vehicles is dead, the plane is useless, and the pilot broke his leg."

"Pilot? You mean Kip?"

"No, this is a pilot from Fort Capstick who flew our new doctor in."

"I didn't even know we had an old doctor."

"Don't ask," I said. "Just take my word for it—it's been a rugged couple of days. Anyway, the bossman wants you to join us for dinner."

"Why?"

"I suppose he wants to talk to you."

"What the hell, he's paying the bills. I suppose one meal a week can't be avoided."

"Where do we meet?"

"Look ahead of you," he said. "Can you see those hills?"

I looked out. "No, I can't see a damned thing. Too much rain and fog."

"Well, trust me, they're about two and a half miles due west of you. You should make them in an hour, even in this slop."

"Then what?"

"I'll have one of my boys leave a trail for you."

"What kind of trail?"

"I don't know—rocks, sticks, whatever it is, you'll recognize it when you come across it. It'll lead you to some caves where we can all stay dry for the night."

"Sounds good to me," I said. "See you at nightfall." I deactivated the radio and turned to Rashid. "Try to keep Crooked Leg away from Kenny and his team. Maybe we can get through the night without his finding out what happened."

"I'll do my best," said Rashid. Suddenly he frowned. "You mentioned his team. How will I identify them?"

"He's got three trackers. They're Orange-Eyes, just like the rest, but they'll be totally naked except for some ornaments. And he's got a couple of Dabih skinners, though I imagine Markham will want them back as soon as it clears up and he can blow more animals away."

Rashid nodded. "I'll leave now."

"Drive for a while," I told him. "Big Shoulders can handle the rain better than you can. It bounces right off that pelt of his."

"I don't want any special treatment. I notice the two cameramen are walking."

"They're more concerned with keeping their equipment dry than themselves," I explained. "You don't see Kip or me with that problem."

"All right."

When I ran back to the first vehicle, I found I had that problem after all. Some of the cargo had shifted when the vehicle did a 360 on the mud, and Kip had moved over to my seat to avoid being crushed.

Everyone had forgotten that I had an artificial leg, and I was too proud—and too mad—to remind them, so I spent the next three hours walking in the driving rain with the cameramen and the Orange-Eyes.

I was feeling a lot less proud, and a lot angrier, when we finally came to a row of caves where Kenny Vaughn was waiting for us.

10

The Men sat huddled in our own cave, which was a little higher and a little better protected from the wind than the caves that were occupied by the Orange-Eyes and the Dabihs.

"Jesus!" muttered Kip, hugging himself with his arms. "I don't think I'm ever going to be dry again."

"I don't remember the rains coming this early," I said to Kenny Vaughn. "How about you?"

He laughed. "You were here for less than a year. I'm surprised you remember anything." He paused thoughtfully. "They came even earlier six years ago."

"You'll stay with us until they stop," said Markham. "It's too easy to get separated in this stuff."

"This is *my* world, Mr. Markham," said Kenny. "I don't get lost on it."

"Yeah, but *we* do. You'll stay with us."

Kenny seemed to be considering Markham's order. Finally

he spoke. "Okay, I'll stick around until you get used to finding your way in the rain. But you're making my job a lot harder. With the rains, the game will be dispersed all the hell over; they won't be hanging around the water holes, where they're easy to find." He paused. "Also, game doesn't stay put. It's always on the move, and you're not likely to keep up with it in this weather, especially missing a vehicle. How did it happen?"

"One of those fucking wags hit a rock that everyone else managed to miss."

"Wags?" asked Kenny, puzzled.

"Orange-Eyes."

Kenny grimaced. "They're not the best drivers in the galaxy. They get bored, and their attention wanders."

"This one won't get bored again," said Markham.

"Oh?"

"Big Shoulders gave him an object lesson he won't forget."

"Yeah, that's probably for the best," said Kenny.

"You don't object?" asked Rashid, who had been totally silent up to that point.

"They're my blood brothers, and I love them—but sometimes they require discipline," answered Kenny.

"This one was pretty badly beaten with a whip," continued Rashid.

"They recover fast," said Kenny. "Besides, I don't think they feel pain the way you and I do. They're lower on the scale."

"What scale?" I demanded.

"Whatever scale you use to measure them against us," answered Kenny, and I realized, for the first time, that even though he'd spent his whole life on Bushveld, associating primarily with Orange-Eyes, that he still thought and reacted like a Man.

"I'm glad we see eye-to-eye on that," said Markham. "Mr. Stone thought you might disapprove."

Kenny shook his head. "There are millions of them and just

a handful of us. You do what you have to do. You can't let them take advantage of you."

"I can't see how wrecking a truck gives the Orange-Eyes an advantage," I said.

"If you don't punish the guilty party, it's a sign of weakness," said Kenny. "You know that, Enoch. And out here in the bush, isolated and outnumbered, you never want give them any reason to think they can question your authority."

I could see I wasn't going to change anyone's mind, so I just shut up and tried to warm myself by the fire that Kenny had built before we arrived.

"What's the penalty for killing an Orange-Eye?" asked Kip.

"Fifty credits," said Kenny.

"Should have shot the bastard," muttered Kip. "I'd have paid for it myself."

"I heard that, Mr. Ngami," said Kenny, and I thought: *Well, he's got a point past which he won't go.* "That's a stupid thing to say."

"Why?" asked Kip belligerently. "He destroyed a truck and a plane through sheer carelessness."

"It's stupid," explained Kenny, "because he's too goddamned hard to replace out here."

"Also, it's murder," I said.

"Execution," Kenny corrected me. "Any Man has the right to do that on safari. You know the law."

"It's murder anyway," I said.

"That museum job's made you soft as putty, Enoch," said Kenny with a smile.

"I've never beaten any being of any race that worked for me," I said.

"That's probably why you lost a leg and never made a reputation," offered Markham. "If you walk the path to greatness, you're going to have to make decisions and commit actions that would be repugnant to normal men."

"I've accomplished a hell of a lot," I said defensively. "I've opened worlds, and had animals and landmarks named after me, and . . ."

"I didn't say you hadn't accomplished anything," said Markham. "I said you haven't sought greatness. To do that, you've got to be more than successful. You have to be *driven*. You've got to have an emptiness . . . a hunger."

"In the pit of the belly?" I asked dryly.

"In the soul," he replied.

"I think I'd rather be me," I said.

"Wait until we get so close to finding Michael Drake that you can almost taste it," said Markham with a knowing smile. "Wait until we're a day away, or an hour, and you're sitting there writing your memoirs and counting your money and fighting off your women, and then tell me if you feel the same."

"We'll see," I said.

Markham turned back to Kenny. "In the meantime, how do we get out of here tomorrow—and where do we go?"

"We dig and we push, of course," responded Kenny. "As for where we go, who knows what's the right direction? All we can do is go from village to village. Some will remember him, some he'll never have visited, and we'll keep adjusting our route with such information as we can obtain." He paused. "As for negotiating the terrain, if the vehicles start sinking in, well, that's what we have Orange-Eyes for. They were pretty full *before* you lost the third one, so lighten them and double the Orange-Eyes' loads. That should make it easier for the vehicles to get through."

"Do we offer them any extra pay?" asked Markham.

"Give 'em an extra credit a day."

"That's all?"

"You don't want to spoil 'em," said Kenny. "Slip Big Shoulders an extra hundred credits. He'll see to it that they don't make any fuss."

"Thank you, Mr. Vaughn," said Markham. "I don't know why we didn't hit it off when we first met. I think we'll get along splendidly from here on."

"I didn't like you then and I don't like you now," said Kenny. "But Men have to stick together."

"Has there ever been a native uprising?" asked Markham.

"Not yet. But then, we haven't incorporated Bushveld into the Democracy yet. We've just got our one little outpost at Fort Capstick. Once someone discovers something that we want on Bushveld and Men start arriving by the thousands, that's when we'll have to pacify them."

"I've seen some worlds after the Navy pacified them," offered Arnaz. "They're not pretty sights."

"So I've been told," said Kenny. He paused. "Well, with a little luck, no one will want to do anything with Bushveld except go hunting here."

"If we find Michael Drake and he's found the cure for ybonia here, the Democracy will move in an hour later," I said. "They'll build laboratories and spaceports and roads and cities, and that will be the end of everyone's way of life."

"It'll take years," said Kenny.

"I've seen what they can do when they're motivated," I replied. "It'll take *months*."

I could see Kenny's concern reflected in his face, and I sympathized with him. In ancient times, when we were still Earthbound, they used elephants to help defoliate the forests and wild places in which they lived, and when they were done the elephants all died from lack of habitat. Kenny had just realized he was being asked to do much the same thing here; if we were successful, neither Bushveld nor Kenny's life would ever be the same again.

11

We had planned to set out at first light the next morning, but during the night the vehicles had sunk into the mud. It took a monumental effort to free them, but after about forty minutes they were proceeding very slowly.

The rain was coming down as hard as the previous day, but now there was a heavy mist in the air, limiting visibility to perhaps half a mile. Men and Orange-Eyes had equal difficulty negotiating the terrain; their feet would sink inches into the mud, then make popping noises as they pulled them out of the holes they had created and made new ones.

Markham decided that he had to walk alongside Kenny, just to prove that he could do it. And now I began to understand that "hunger" he spoke about, for though Kenny was young and fit and a native to Bushveld, and Markham was middle-aged and out of shape, he matched Kenny stride for stride, and was still going strong when Kenny called a rest break. I think it was only the fact that it was demeaning for Men to carry loads that stopped Markham from proving to Big Shoulders that he could carry more weight than any Orange-Eye in the party.

"He looks happy," noted Kip, who was sitting in the back of my vehicle.

"The life agrees with him," I said.

"Bullshit. This life doesn't agree with anyone. The *challenge* agrees with him."

"Yeah, I suppose so," I agreed. "Still, anything that puts him in a good mood is okay by me."

"If Kenny takes him hunting, he can blow away half a dozen innocent animals," offered Kip. "*That* ought to keep him happy."

We got bogged down again just then, and I hopped out while the Orange-Eyes rocked the vehicle, trying to get it free of the mud.

It seemed like a good time to check on Stuart and Crooked Leg. It turned out that the Orange-Eye was one of those rocking and pushing the vehicle. Even though I had been on Bushveld before, and had worked with Orange-Eyes before, I couldn't help marveling at the vitality of these strange beings. Any Man I knew would have been laid up for weeks or possibly even months from a similar beating.

Stuart seemed to be in considerable pain as the vehicle shook and lurched over the rugged terrain.

"How are you holding up?" I asked.

"Lousy," he replied. "How far to the next village?"

I shrugged. "I've no idea. But Kenny knows you need help, and he knows the territory better than anyone."

"Kenny Vaughn?"

"You know him?" I asked.

"Of course I know him. How many Men do you think there *are* on Bushveld?" He paused. "Does Kenny know when we'll make the next village?"

"I spoke to him during breakfast. The tribes in this area are semi-nomadic; they've got villages all over, and they move from one to another, following the best grazing for their animals. So there's no way we can pinpoint them on a map. But their territory isn't endless. They make a circuit, and we should come across some of them before too long."

"When is that?"

"I don't know," I answered. "Maybe a day or two, maybe a little longer."

"Then I'm going to need more painkillers."

"You can tell the doctor yourself," I said. "He'll be checking on you every hour."

"He hates me. I know him from when he used to work on Bushveld."

"He doesn't strike me as the type who hates anyone," I said.

"You're the expedition leader," said Stuart. "I want you tell Rashid I have to have more painkillers."

"I'll do what I can," I said.

I left him and walked through the driving rain to Rashid, who was standing some distance away, as if he was afraid someone might see him and ask him to help rock the vehicle out of the mud.

"I just talked to your patient," I said.

"I know. I saw you."

"He asked me to ask you for—"

"Painkillers," interrupted Rashid. "I know."

"So . . . can you give him some?"

"He's loaded with them. You could stick a knife into him and he probably wouldn't feel it."

"Then what . . . ?"

"The man's been an addict for at least five years," replied Rashid. "He doesn't want painkillers, he wants hallucinogens. Now, it happens that the medication for a couple of local diseases contains what he wants, and he's been on Bushveld long enough to know it. *That's* what he's angling for."

"Then why did you let him pilot you out here?"

"He was the only pilot available," he replied with a shrug. "And I checked the drug levels in his blood back at Fort Capstick before I agreed to get into the plane."

Wonderful, I thought. *It's not enough that I have to deal with Markham, and that Kenny's managed to tarnish his Great White Hunter image forever, and Kip wants to kill an Orange-Eye, and we've lost a vehicle and a plane. Now we're stuck with a junkie as well. Just great.*

I walked over to Kenny, who was standing next to Markham, watching the Orange-Eyes try to dig the vehicle out of the mud. "Any idea where the next village might be?"

"Not far," he said. "Grazing looks pretty good. They'll be around here."

"Why? I mean, if the grazing's good here, why not assume it's just as good fifty or a hundred miles from here?"

"It probably is."

"Then why do you think we're close to a village?" I persisted.

"Because if they take their cattle a hundred miles from here, they'll be attacked by a rival tribe. Their borders are elastic, but not infinite."

"We've got to get to a village pretty soon," I said.

"The pilot?"

"Yes."

"We'll do our best. Of course, finding a village will be a lot easier than convincing the Orange-Eyes to care for him until he can be transported back to Fort Capstick."

"Why?" asked Markham. "We don't have any problem with the Orange-Eyes you supplied."

"They're half-civilized," answered Kenny. "We've even got them on a monied economy. But the bulk of their race has never seen a Man—or, if they have, they have good reason not to want to do us any favors." He paused. "Still, if Michael Drake passed through here, we should be all right."

"And if he didn't?" asked Markham.

"Then I'll have to find out what's valuable to them, and negotiate. Salt or meat usually does the trick."

Just then the vehicle came free with a loud sucking sound, and we were soon back on the road again—though of course there was nothing resembling a road any closer than Fort Capstick. After about an hour we came to an area where, though the rain persisted, the natural drainage was much better, and we managed to go almost five miles before we got stuck again.

This time both vehicles were bogged down, and Kenny, seeing some herbivores watching us curiously from a distance, decided it was time to shoot something for dinner before visibility got even worse.

"I've never seen one of these animals before," said Markham. "I'd like one for a trophy."

"They're called Cochrane's Hornbuck, and there's not a trophy animal in the batch," replied Kenny, instructing his lenses to focus on the herd. "You want at least sixteen-inch horns."

"How can you tell?" demanded Markham. "They're five hundred yards away."

"Look at the ears," said Kenny. "Never yet saw a hornbuck with ears more than six inches long. None of these animals has horns that are more than twice the length of its ears." He smiled at Markham. "It's a hunter's shorthand. If your cameramen take you shooting one of these, you'll be a laughingstock among anyone who knows the species."

"Ah," said Markham with a sly smile. "But no one beyond Bushveld does."

"Just wait," said Kenny. "We'll get you one to be proud of. But what we need now is dinner."

He took his laser rifle from his gunbearer, then raised, aimed, and fired it all in one motion. One of the hornbucks leaped ten feet in the air, wheeled as it landed, and raced off in the opposite direction. It ran about eighty yards, then dropped as if it had run into a wall.

Kenny turned to his tracker and said something in the Orange-Eyes' language. The tracker repeated it to three others, and then the four Orange-Eyes trotted across the plain to where the hornbuck had fallen, picked it up, and carried it back on their shoulders.

"We can make a few more miles today," Kenny told Markham. "There's no sense hanging the hornbuck. I'll have them take it down the trail a bit and bleed it there. The Dabihs can skin it, too," he added. "You never know who might want to trade for a nice pelt."

"Do we have time?"

"They'll be done before you get your vehicles unstuck."

He turned and uttered a terse command to his Orange-Eyes, who carried the hornbuck off. Another command and the Dabihs fell into step behind them.

It took almost an hour this time to free the vehicles, and poor Stuart had to share his space with the dead hornbuck, which no longer had any blood or skin. We couldn't chop it up into small pieces that the Orange-Eyes could carry, because that would have attracted every insect and, more important, every carnivore in the area, so we stuck it on the vehicle and covered it with a tarp.

We made camp after we'd covered another ten miles—good progress considering the rain and the mud—but unlike the previous night, we didn't have the comfort of caves. The humans stayed inside the vehicles while the Orange-Eyes set up our bubbles, then quickly moved into them. Stuart claimed he was in too much pain to be moved without more drugs, but when Markham said that he'd have to remain in the vehicle all night, he changed his mind and allowed some Orange-Eyes to carry him into a bubble.

In the middle of the night I woke up, sweating and trembling. I knew from past experience that it was jungle fever coming on, and I sent for Rashid, who gave me a couple of pills that seemed to concentrate all the pain in my stomach. I vomited a few times, suffered through a serious bout of diarrhea, then went back to sleep, and felt much healthier, if somewhat weaker, in the morning.

It was still raining when we broke camp after breakfast—which I chose not to eat, just to be on the safe side—and headed off through a heavy mist. Kenny sent two of his trackers ahead to see if they could spot any game. They returned about two hours later with the news that there was a village up ahead.

"About a mile," said Kenny, translating. "They didn't make contact, since they're not from the local tribe and they didn't want to risk being attacked."

"Why won't they attack *us?*" asked Markham.

"We're a different species, not a rival tribe," I explained. "It's much easier for a Man to approach an Orange-Eye village than it is for an Orange-Eye."

Markham looked to Kenny for confirmation.

"Enoch's right," he said. "He's been here before. He knows how things work."

"That's what I hired him for," said Markham. "But you're the native; it never hurts to double-check."

I kept my resentment to myself, because while he may have been an insensitive bastard, he was also absolutely right: it made perfect sense to double-check with someone who'd lived here all his life.

"Well, at least we'll get rid of the pilot," said Markham at last. "Let's get going."

We climbed back into the vehicles and followed the two trackers as they walked along, leading the way through the rain. After about half a mile I started peering into the mist, wondering where the village was. The vehicle began hydroplaning, and just as I was sure it was going to get stuck again, it suddenly straightened out and kept moving.

And then, materializing miraculously through the mist, the village appeared directly ahead of us—the same square huts in the same geometric pattern. It was a large village, too: there were at least fifty huts, with a borehole for water in the center, where it was convenient to all the inhabitants. Surrounding the village were dozens of thorn corrals for their meat animals.

As we approached, I sensed something was wrong. For a moment I couldn't put my finger on it, and then I realized that nothing was moving. Not in the village, not in the corrals, not anywhere.

I sprang out of the vehicle and moved ahead of the trackers, Screecher in hand. Kenny joined me an instant later, as did Markham.

"What the hell happened here?" asked Markham.

"I don't know yet," said Kenny.

We reached the village. The stench of dead Orange-Eyes was sickening, and the sight that met our eyes was even worse. Every male, female, and child Orange-Eye had been mutilated and killed.

"Who did this?" asked Markham, signaling Kerr and Arnaz to bring their cameras.

Kenny looked off into the mist at something only he could see.

"The same Orange-Eyes who are watching us right now," he answered.

12

I peered through the mist, and finally saw a slight movement.

"Get back!" ordered Kenny, and I retreated to the shadow of our vehicle.

"What's going on?" demanded Markham.

"We've intruded on a private little genocide," said Kenny. "If we don't show any signs of aggression, maybe they'll let us go back the way we came. It depends on whether they've had any dealings with the colonial government."

"I don't follow you."

"If they know that Men are running this planet, then they know we'll exact some serious retribution for what they've done if we can identify them—and there's no way in hell they're going to let us go back and report what we've seen. If they *don't* know about Men, well then, we're not a tribal enemy, and as long as we don't look like we're spoiling for a fight, they'll probably let us pass."

"How will we know?" asked Markham.

"If they start throwing spears, they know who we are," answered Kenny grimly.

Kip climbed out of the vehicle and peered into the mist. "Can you make out their tribal totem?"

Kenny shook his head. "If I could, I might know what they planned to do next." He squinted. "Hell, I can't even make out their figures."

"Well, we can't stay here all day waiting for them to make up their minds," said Markham. "Once night falls, we're at their mercy."

"Sometimes waiting is the very best thing to do," said Kenny. "If we turn back, they'll be sure we're going to report them to Fort Capstick."

"They've probably never heard of Fort Capstick," said Markham.

"Even so, they could view it as a retreat and read it as a sign of weakness."

"So we go forward."

"That could be a sign of aggression."

"What are they armed with?" asked Markham.

"Spears, clubs, knives, maybe some bows and arrows."

"You mean to say you're going to let some savages with clubs dictate what we do?" demanded Markham.

"There could be a couple of thousand of them," answered Kenny. "They sure as hell wiped out the village without much of a struggle."

"This is ridiculous!" snapped Markham. He raised his laser rifle to his shoulder.

"What are you doing?" demanded Kenny.

"They want aggression, I'll give them aggression," said Markham, firing into the mist. "No goddamned tribe of savages is going to dictate what *I* do!"

Kenny grabbed at the barrel of Markham's rifle, but Markham simply turned and sprayed the area with killing beams of solid light. Before Kenny finally wrestled the gun from him, we heard a number of screams coming from the mist.

"You idiot!" bellowed Kenny. "Now we're in for it!"

"Unless you plan to hold them off by yourself," said Markham calmly, "I think you'd be well-advised to return my rifle to me and start ordering our wags to take up a defensive position."

Kenny glared at him with murder in his eye, but realized he was right. He handed Markham back his gun, then began giving orders to the Orange-Eyes in their native tongue. They spread out in a semicircle behind the vehicles. Most didn't even have spears, and they searched the ground for rocks that they could throw or use in hand-to-hand combat.

"What about the cameramen?" asked Kenny. "Do they know how to use weapons?"

"They'll be much too busy to participate," said Markham.

"Busy?" repeated Kenny. "Doing what?"

"Making a record of the battle to come."

"Fat lot of good it'll do if we lose."

"We have guns," said Markham confidently. "The enemy has sticks and stones."

"We have about half a dozen guns," said Kenny. "They have about a million sticks and stones—and we can't see them in this pea soup."

"If we can't see them, they can't see us," said Markham. He turned to Kip. "Mr. Ngami, go about fifty yards to your left." Then, to me: "Mr. Stone, go off to the right. No, don't look to Mr. Vaughn for his approval; this is *my* expedition." I did as he ordered; to this day I don't know why. But so did Kip, and a moment later we were where he wanted us.

"All right," continued Markham. "On my signal, I want each

of you to begin sweeping the area in front of you with your weapons. Mr. Vaughn and I will shoot at any movement your fire precipitates."

"Just the four of us against however many hundreds of them there are?" I asked.

"We can't risk Mr. Rashid," said Markham. "We may have need of medical treatment later. As for Mr. Stuart, he's in no condition to help us."

"And what do you propose to do when they all charge down upon the four of us?" demanded Kenny.

"Teach them a lesson the survivors will never forget," said Markham with no trace of fear or even apprehension. He looked first at Kip, then at me. "Gentlemen—fire!"

We began sweeping the area. There were a few more screams, but no motion.

Kenny stared dead ahead, frowning, and I knew what he was thinking: Even if they'd never seen a gun before, they knew now how much damage we could do. Why hadn't they either charged when they saw there were only four armed Men, or else taken off to safer parts? Why were we still able to make a few lucky hits without eliciting a response?

And then we both figured it out at the same instant.

"Kip!" yelled Kenny. "Watch the back door!"

No sooner had the words left his mouth than some two hundred Orange-Eyes who had circled around under the protective cover of the mist charged down from behind us, screaming their war cries. Three of our own Orange-Eyes broke and ran, and were brutally skewered within seconds.

I limped over to help Kip hold them off—my prosthetic leg was acceptable for walking, even through the mud, but the faster I tried to move the worse my limp became—and I could tell from the screams behind me that another batch of them were charging down from the village.

I heard a grunt of pain and surprise, but I was too busy to even turn and see what had happened. Kip lay on his belly, shooting as quickly as he could spot the enemy. I was afraid that if I knelt or lay down, my leg wouldn't respond when I wanted to rise again, so I propped myself up against the vehicle, aimed my rifle across the hood, and started firing.

I could hear Markham cursing behind me. I figured as long as I could hear him he was alive and didn't need my help as much as Kip did, because as quickly as we mowed the Orange-Eyes down, more moved forward to take their places.

Once we got in rhythm, one recharging as the other fired, it was a slaughter. There were hundreds of them, and they came at us fearlessly, but one spray with a Burner or a Screecher could bring down fifteen to twenty of them in less than two seconds. Also—to their detriment in this case—they'd been well schooled in war, enough to know that you can't reload a spear, that once you hurl it it's gone. None of them got close enough to thrust a spear into either of us, and even when they got within twenty yards of Kip or me, they still refused to hurl their spears but clung to them as we methodically mowed them down.

A few managed to get past our killing zone. Mostly they came from behind us, and Big Shoulders directed our Orange-Eyes against them. Those battles were brutal and bloody, hand-to-hand between creatures schooled in the same weapons, but our Orange-Eyes greatly outnumbered those who got close enough to threaten us and made quick if messy work of them.

Finally there were no more Orange-Eyes left to kill, and after a tense moment of scanning the battlefield for further threats, we relaxed and lowered our weapons.

"By God, we did it!" exclaimed Kip, almost giggling with relief.

"And we captured it all for posterity!" chimed in Kerr, climbing down from his perch atop the second vehicle.

"And without a single casualty!" I added.

"Wrong," said Markham. "We had one casualty."

"Oh?" I turned and walked over to him.

"Mr. Vaughn."

I looked down and saw Kenny's body, spattered with mud and blood, half-buried beneath a pair of Orange-Eyes, a spear protruding from his chest, his head crushed by a stone.

"Shit!" I said, kneeling down to search futilely for signs of life.

Rashid came over and briefly examined him. "He was probably dead before he hit the ground."

Kip glared at Markham with undisguised hostility. "Well, you did it this time!" he spat.

"We won the battle," said Markham. "There was only one casualty. We must have killed close to six hundred of the enemy, maybe more. It's unfortunate, and I'm sorry it happened, but Mr. Vaughn represents a statistically acceptable loss."

"You don't understand," said Kip. "You killed a few hundred members of a nameless tribe. For all you know, there are ten thousand more, and now that they know what our guns can do, they're probably preparing an ambush twenty miles up the road. And because you opened fire on them, we lost the only man who's lived with them, who could speak their language and knew how they think." He paused, then added bitterly, "He was also the only man who could feed this goddamned safari."

Markham stared at him coldly. "Are you quite finished, Mr. Ngami?"

"For the moment."

"All right," said Markham, looking around. "Mr. Ngami, you are now our meat hunter."

"I've never hunted in my life," said Kip.

"Then learn. You're what we can spare."

"Enoch knows how," protested Kip. "Let *him* do the hunting."

"That's out of the question. Mr. Stone is the only Man who's been to Bushveld before. He knows a little of the language, and he's dealt with some of the Orange-Eyes before." He paused. "You, on the other hand, have no other function with this expedition, now that the plane has been destroyed. You're our meat hunter. Take Mr. Vaughn's trackers and skinners with you." He stared at Kip. "And since we don't want you getting hopelessly lost, you'll stay in radio contact with us every two hours, and join us each evening when we make camp."

"You could get awfully hungry," said Kip.

"Nonsense. Those are experienced trackers, and you're not a sportsman who's trying to give the animals an even chance to get away or attack you. Just take a Burner and a Screecher and kill whatever we need to eat as quickly and efficiently as possible. Since we're not going to be keeping skins as trophies, we won't need the Dabihs for that, so let them be your porters."

"Porters?" asked Kip.

"They can be your gunbearers during the hunt, and they can carry the meat back to camp after you've killed it. Take Mr. Vaughn's weapons, have Big Shoulders tell the trackers that they're working for you now, and make sure you take a communicator that works."

He turned to me. "Tell Cotton Jacket to put together a crew to dig a grave for Mr. Vaughn."

"What about the three dead Orange-Eyes?" I asked.

"They're just wags," said Markham. "Do with them what you want."

"They're wags who died for you," I pointed out.

"I said to do what you want," said Markham coldly. "If they get buried, bury them. If they get cremated, burn them. If they get left out for the animals and the insects to eat, leave them out. Just don't bother me about it." He frowned. "And take that ridiculous arrow out of your leg."

I looked down, and saw for the first time that I'd taken an

arrow in my prosthetic leg. I yanked it out, and was about to throw it onto the mud when Rashid came up to me.

"May I have it, please?" he asked.

"What for?" demanded Markham.

"I want to check the tip for poison," answered Rashid. "If they're using any, perhaps I can identify it and synthesize an antidote."

Markham considered for a moment. "Will something that poisons Orange-Eyes be dangerous to a Man? I mean, our metabolisms are very different."

"I won't know until I set up a field lab," said Rashid. "But we're both oxygen-breathing mammals, and I have a feeling that if it's effective against them, it could be equally deadly to *us*."

Markham nodded his approval. "It can't hurt, and all you've got to do is keep Stuart alive, so you certainly have enough time on your hands."

"I've got about forty Orange-Eyes to patch up," Rashid corrected him.

"Let them take care of themselves," said Markham. "I'm paying you to care for the Men in this expedition."

"They risked their lives in your service," said Rashid bluntly. "I think the least you can do is allow them access to my services."

"I've been on worlds like this before," said Markham. "If you don't draw a distinct line in the dirt between you and the natives, before long you weigh three hundred pounds, you stop bathing, and you want to marry one of them."

"I don't want to marry anyone," said Rashid. "I just want to patch up their wounds."

"I don't believe you heard a word I said," replied Markham irritably. "The answer is no."

"There are a couple who won't be able to continue if I don't help them."

"Damn it! I said—"

"Just a minute, Mr. Markham," I interrupted. "If they think they're expendable, they could all desert some night. Why not let him work on the ones who are in the worst shape? It would be a gesture they'd understand—and there may come a day when we need every last one of them."

He thought about it for a moment, then turned back to Rashid. "All right," he said. "But just the ones who couldn't continue on their own."

Rashid didn't bother to thank him, but immediately headed off toward the wounded Orange-Eyes before Markham could change his mind.

A few moments later Cotton Jacket reported that the grave was ready, and I had a pair of Orange-Eyes carry Kenny's body over to it. We laid him in it and covered him with mud. Then Markham suggested that we place a cross over it.

"Bad idea," I said.

"Why?"

"I don't know anything about the Orange-Eyes who killed him. For all I know they might want to dig up him and mutilate his body. Why tell them where it is?"

"Has that actually happened on Bushveld?" asked Markham.

"A few times, or so I've been told."

"Good. After dinner I'll get my recorder and you can tell me everything you know about the practice."

"You don't have enough articles for one day?" I asked, looking around and surveying the carnage.

"The public has a voracious appetite, Mr. Stone."

"Let 'em come out here with us and I'll bet they'd be sated soon enough."

"We're here precisely because they won't come. They'd rather enjoy our experiences vicariously."

"*Enjoy?*" I said. "We've had one Man killed, another is probably dying, one of our vehicles has broken down, we've fought off one attack and may be facing another at any moment, and you call that enjoyable?"

"*I* call it exciting," Markham corrected me. "My readers call it enjoyable. Either way, it works."

It was not the first time I wondered if he was simply too brave by half, or out-and-out crazy.

13

Kenny Vaughn's death seemed to mark a turning point in our journey.

The rains grew even worse, and progress was almost nil. There was no game to be found, at least by Kip and his trackers. More than two dozen of our Orange-Eyes came down with some debilitating disease that Rashid couldn't even name, let alone cure, and we actually lost four of them before it had run its course.

I don't think we made five miles a day, and we were constantly on guard against another attack. We saw frequent signs that we were not alone, but for whatever reason, the local tribe kept its distance. At first we were grateful, but as the days passed and we realized just how vulnerable we were, crippled with illness and ankle-deep in mud, their absence began to bother us even more. We knew they were going to attack again sooner or later, and we couldn't understand why they held off.

"How large an area can they control?" asked Markham during one rest break. "Is it possible we're through it already?"

"I doubt it," I said. "We can't be thirty miles from the spot where they killed Kenny. A tribe as numerous as this one could control a hundred or more miles in each direction."

"Each direction from *where?*" persisted Markham. "Maybe we were on the outskirts of their territory when they attacked, and we're out of it now."

"Maybe," I said. "But we keep coming across *somebody's* tracks."

"Why should they be made by the same tribe that attacked us?"

"Because it's the only tribe in this area that knows how powerful our weapons are," I answered. "They're the only ones who have good reason to keep their distance."

"I don't like it," he muttered. "We've got to do something about them."

"If I were you," I countered, "I'd be more concerned about the weather. At the rate we're going, it could take a couple of lifetimes just to find out if Michael Drake is on Bushveld."

"He's here, all right," said Markham. "I feel it in my bones."

"All *I* feel is wet," I said.

"Could be worse," said Markham.

"Yeah? How?"

"Could be snow," he said. "I spent a year on Snowball. Ever hear of it?"

"Nope."

"It's in the Willowby Cluster, about the same size as Bushveld. Except that the entire world is one giant glacier. The whole time I was there the temperature never once got above minus-twenty degrees Celsius."

"What the hell were you doing there for a whole year?" I asked.

"I spent the first half year living with Snowmen, and—"

"Snowmen?" I interrupted. "What are *they?*"

"Mutated men," he answered. "Well, 'mutated' is probably the wrong word, since it implies a natural change. These are Men three and four generations removed from the original colonists, whose genes have been rearranged to help them adapt to Snowball. Their bones and muscles are able to withstand the heavier gravity, their fur protects them from the bitter cold, they can metabolize the food they find on the world . . ."

"What food?" I said. "I thought you said it was all a glacier."

"Certain hardy plants live in sheltered valleys, and there are quite a few animals, all evolved on Snowball and of course totally adapted to it—especially in the oceans."

"So you spent six months studying the Snowmen. What about the rest of the time?"

"Arnaz and I went out after Yetis."

"What's a Yeti?"

"In Earth mythology, it's the Abominable Snowman. But on Snowball, it's a two-legged carnivore that was at the top of the food chain before the Snowmen got there. It's about twelve feet tall, and its agility is almost unbelievable. There were never very many of them; they're such good predators that the shortage of prey kept their numbers down. They resented the coming of the Snowmen, and most of them were killed in what almost amounted to a war between the two races. Now there are less than two hundred left, and they're a protected species." He smiled grimly at the memory. "They, on the other hand, don't think of Man as a protected species. Arnaz and I had some narrow escapes. In fact, I finally had to kill a couple of them to save our lives. The fine cost me half of what I made during the year."

I slapped at an orange-and-blue insect that was nibbling painfully on the side of my neck, and pulled another pair out of my hair.

"I could do with an iceworld right about now," I said bitterly.

"Go there and then tell me that," said Markham with the

smug air of One Who Knows lecturing One Who Merely Imagines.

Suddenly Cotton Jacket ran up to me.

"What is it?" I asked.

"There is a village just over the next hill!" he said excitedly.

"How do you know?" I asked, for all the trackers were with Kip, and none of our Orange-Eyes dared to stray too far from the caravan.

"Ngami has returned," he said, pointing to Kip, who had rejoined the main group while Markham and I were talking. "He has seen it."

"Kip!" I called, and he walked over a moment later.

"Mr. Ngami," said Markham, "I understand you've found a village?"

"Right," said Kip. "Maybe two miles ahead."

"Deserted?"

Kip shook his head. "No, it's full of Orange-Eyes."

"Did *they* see *you?*" asked Markham.

"Yes."

"And they didn't attack or run away?"

"No. They just stared at us."

"Did you see their totem?" I asked. "Is it the same as the Orange-Eyes who attacked us?"

"I didn't get that close," said Kip. "Hell, I'm the only one who was armed."

"Well, they didn't attack," mused Markham. "That's something, anyway."

"You want to chance it?" I asked.

"I think we have to," said Markham.

"Why press our luck?" said Kip. "If we give it a wide berth, maybe they'll leave us alone. If we march right up to it, it's going to look like an act of agression."

"We don't have any choice, Mr. Ngami," said Markham.

"Of course we have a choice," responded Kip. "We can march around it."

Markham shook his head. "We've got to leave Mr. Stuart there."

"He's survived this long," said Kip. "Why not take him with us until we know we're out of hostile territory?"

"Because it may extend for hundreds of miles," said Markham, "and our progress with the vehicles is unacceptable. I plan to leave them, and most of our supplies, behind, and proceed on foot. We'll make much faster time."

"On *foot?*" Kip and I said in unison.

"Right. We'll take the bubbles and the medical supplies, dump the rest, and live off the land. But we can't take Stuart. If we leave the vehicles behind, we've got to leave *him,* too."

"But why leave the vehicles?"

"They're spending more time stuck than moving. We're doing about six or seven miles a day, tops. I think we can march twenty."

"It'll still take you a lifetime to circumvent Bushveld," I warned him.

"We'll take our radios. When the rain stops, we'll send for planes and wheels."

"What makes you think they'll care for Stuart, even if they don't attack us?" asked Kip.

"We'll simply convince them that it's in their best interest," said Markham so coldly that I had to repress an involuntary shudder.

When the break was over we marched directly toward the village. When we reached it, Markham ordered me and Big Shoulders to accompany him, and the three of us entered the place. They had been waiting for us, and we walked between two rows of spear-carrying warriors until we came to an old Orange-Eye sitting on a stool.

"Translate for me," said Markham to Big Shoulders, who

nodded. "Greetings, Venerable One. We come in peace and friendship."

Big Shoulders repeated it in the Orange-Eye dialect. The old Orange-Eye made no response.

"We have gifts for you," continued Markham.

"Where are they?" asked the old Orange-Eye.

"We will present them to you shortly," said Markham. "But first we have a favor to ask of you."

The old Orange-Eye stared at him but said nothing.

"One of our companions is badly injured, and cannot continue our journey. We would like to leave him in your care until the rains have ended and some members of my race arrive to take him back home."

"We do not know how to care for one of you," said the Orange-Eye.

"Before I leave, we will show you," said Markham.

"And if we refuse?"

"You will not refuse."

"Why not?"

"Because if he is not alive when his friends come to take him home, not a single dwelling in your village will be left standing, and not a single member of it will remain alive."

"Those are bold threats to come from such a small party," said the old Orange-Eye.

"There are far more than three of us," responded Markham. "Some of our party is just outside the village, and thousands more are only a few miles away."

"That was stupid," I said. "He's the chief. This is his land. He'll know you're lying."

"No choice," shot back Markham. "The truth wasn't going to frighten anyone."

"We will care for him," said the chief promptly. "Now let us see your presents."

"Fine," said Markham. He turned to Big Shoulders. "Bring

some salt and some of the other things we brought to trade, and also have Stuart brought here on a litter. Oh, and have Dr. Rashid come along as well."

Big Shoulders grunted an affirmative and went off in search of the salt and Stuart, while Markham turned to me.

"You see?" he said. "The chief has already agreed."

"He agreed too quickly," I said. "He should have demanded to see your presents and then asked for double the amount to care for Stuart."

"Nonsense," replied Markham. "He obviously knows what our weapons can do, and he's determined to avoid having his people massacred."

I shook my head. "If he's had reports about our weapons, then he knows only four of us used them. Kenny's dead, and you and I are here in his village, unarmed. All he had to do was have his warriors spear us, and there's no way Kip could hold off his army, however small it might be."

"Then let's add a closing argument," said Markham.

He withdrew his Burner, and had a couple of our Orange-Eyes roll a huge stone to the middle of the village.

When he had everyone's attention, he trained the Burner on the rock, turned it to High Intensity, and squeezed the trigger. Within half a minute the huge rock had been reduced to a glowing red puddle.

"If anything happens to our friend," announced Markham, "I will return and use this weapon on every member of the village." He pointed it at the chief. "Starting with you."

The chief swallowed hard.

14

The old Orange-Eye actually wined and dined us, during which time Markham made quite a production about radioing Stuart's situation and location to Fort Capstick. As we left the chief made quite a show of posting guards around the hut where we had deposited Stuart.

"You see?" said Markham as we walked through the forest. "A little show of force was all it took."

"I hope you're right," I said dubiously.

Markham summoned Cotton Jacket, and put the question to him: "What will happen to Stuart once those Orange-Eyes know we aren't coming back?"

Cotton Jacket shrugged. "Maybe they kill him. Maybe they just let him die."

"Even though I promised them more presents if they kept him alive long enough for a medical team from Fort Capstick to reach him?"

"They will tell doctors they do their best, but he die anyway, and they will demand presents for their efforts," answered Cotton Jacket.

"Why didn't you say something while we were in the village?" demanded Markham.

"He is just a Man, and he is dying anyway."

For a moment I thought Markham would strike him, but the moment passed, and finally he just shrugged and started walking again. "Duplicitous bastards," he muttered. "Still, we can't go back and sit with him until help arrives. It could be weeks. And I can't leave Rashid. If they kill Stuart, they'll kill him too; and even if they don't, *we* may need a medic before this expedition's over, and there are a lot more of us than of Stuart." He sighed. "Let's hope Cotton Jacket's wrong." Suddenly he grimaced. "I don't suppose there *are* any noble races in the galaxy. Just an occasional misguided noble individual."

"Misguided?"

"Nobility doesn't pay all that well, Michael Drake excepted." Another grin. "And it's ignoble men like me who exploit them and bring them to public notice."

"I think Michael Drake would be known in any age," I said. "He didn't need the press."

"*Everyone* needs the press," said Markham, wiping some rain from his face, which was wet again before he had finished. "Hell, the average citizen can't tell you who his planetary governor is, or pick out his world on a map of the local systems. He doesn't go one step out of his way to learn *anything*. Without the press to tell him what to think, he wouldn't think at all."

"You don't have a terribly high opinion of the people who keep you in business, do you?" I asked.

"Why do you think I hunt up sensational stories?" he shot back. "I could do a well-reasoned article on the benefits that would accrue if the galactic economy went to a platinum standard, but only six people would read it, and four of them wouldn't give a damn anyway. But hunt a Yeti, or find Michael Drake, and billions are enthralled."

"That's a hell of a cynical attitude to tote through life," I noted.

"I didn't make the rules," answered Markham. "I just play by them."

Markham had sent Kerr off with Kip to photograph any charging animals—there was no reason for a small herbivore to charge its pursuers, but Markham explained that exciting things happen whether there's a camera handy or not, so we might as well have one. Arnaz, who had picked up some kind of skin fungus that Rashid was treating, stayed behind; in fact, we rigged up a litter so two of the Orange-Eyes could carry him through the mud, despite his protests that he didn't need any help. Since Markham spoke only Terran, and I was the only Man available, we walked and talked together as we proceeded farther and farther along the barely discernible trail leading from the village.

He never knew his father, and his mother had died when he was only five. He'd been shunted from one distant relative to another until he ran off as a young teenager. He made his way as a thief and a con man until his late teens. He was always brighter than his cronies, and he finally decided, at nineteen, to go back to school. He falsified his records, got into a college on Abacus II, edited the school newstape, and graduated with honors at twenty-two.

He returned to the world where he'd been a youthful thief—he never told me its name—got a job as a reporter, and won an award and a handsome raise for exposing all his former buddies. While he was traveling to Clearwater III, the capital world of his sector, to pick up the award, the spaceliner that was ferrying him had some faulty sensors and was hit by a meteor. It would have been all right if the crew hadn't panicked and ignored the proper procedure for getting a crippled ship safely to port. Eighty-three passengers died, but Markham had the presence of mind to make his way to one of the landing shuttles and seal himself inside it, using its supply of oxygen to keep alive while he radioed the dying ship's position over and over until it was picked up.

The reward for *that* story, which was syndicated all over the Democracy, made Markham an overnight celebrity. In fact, it was so much more than the amount he received for his first story that he decided the fame and money he coveted could best be gotten by a single-minded pursuit of the sensational, which he proceeded to do.

He'd had five or six successes over the years—and because of the nature of the truly sensational, twice that many failures, which only made him more determined to succeed the next time. He'd done some interesting work, some good work, and some popular work—but now he wanted to do some *important* work.

"I don't want to just be remembered as the man who shot a Yeti, or climbed Mount Prekana without an oxygen mask," he confided as we walked along the muddy trail. "If I can bring Michael Drake back to the Democracy, if I can present millions of victims with a cure for ybonia, I'll have my place in history."

"Do you need one?" I asked.

"Do you believe in God?" he asked in turn.

"Not often," I admitted.

"Neither do I. Not ever. But I believe in immortality."

"You must have fun reconciling that with your atheism," I commented dryly.

"I don't believe in the kind of immortality you're thinking of, and I don't believe in any eternal afterlife. But I believe if you make a mark to show you were here, and someone comes across that mark after you're gone, you're alive again for the moment it takes him to look at it." He paused. "I've written some good things, but they're ephemeral—of the moment. But if I can bring back Michael Drake and write up the adventure we're undergoing . . . hell, people will be reading it and talking about it for five hundred years, and every time they do I'll be alive again. *That's* my immortality."

"I don't know if putting your immortality in the hands of a bunch of readers who haven't been born yet is any better than hoping there's a God and letting Him take care of it," I replied.

He just stared at me for a moment, rain dripping down his face, and then continued foot-slogging through the muck.

We made camp in late afternoon, and waited for Kip and his trackers and skinners to show up with dinner. They finally caught up with us about four hours later.

"What the hell kept you?" demanded Markham.

"I'm not Kenny Vaughn," said Kip. "He could down a brownbuck at half a mile. Me, I have to get within two hundred yards to make sure of my shot, and if you know how to sneak up on a brownbuck quietly when your feet make sucking sounds every time you pull them out of the mud, I wish you'd tell me."

"So did you shoot anything or not?"

Kip signaled the Dabihs, who carried a pair of brownbuck carcasses over and dropped them on the ground at Markham's feet.

"If it's so difficult, why did you shoot two of them?" demanded Markham.

"I figured I might not get close enough to kill one tomorrow. The second one's meat'll keep for twenty-four hours."

"You're not thinking, Kip," I said. "It's not a matter of the meat keeping, but of how many predators the smell of fresh meat will draw."

"I hadn't considered that," he admitted. Then he smiled. "Tell you what: I'll hang the second one from a tree, set up a blind, and shoot a couple of Hooktooths and Killerdogs. Where does it say we can't eat predators?"

"As long as we eat them before they eat us," said Markham.

"Just stay in your bubble and nothing'll bother you," said Kip.

"I hope not," replied Markham, getting to his feet. "I've got an article to prepare. Have Cotton Jacket bring me my dinner when it's ready."

He walked off toward his bubble, and Kip sat down on his chair. I called Big Shoulders over, told him to prepare one of the carcasses for dinner and hang the other in a tree. Big Shoulders gave him a curious stare and then followed his orders.

"So how do you like the hunting biz?" I asked when the brownbucks had been removed.

"Beats the hell out of being near Markham."

"When did you kill the two bucks?"

Kip looked around to make sure no one else was listening, then grinned. "About noontime."

"I figured."

"How could you tell?"

"The broken leg on the one you hung," I said. "I figure you already bled the one we're going to eat."

He grinned. "You're pretty quick on the uptake."

"Thanks. My guess is that rigor had set in on the other and you decided that even Markham would be bright enough to dope out that you'd killed them hours ago and just didn't want to share his company—so you broke the legs and figured he wouldn't spot the stiff necks."

"It was that or tell him we spent eight hours looking for camp, and considering that I've got Kenny's trackers with me, I didn't think he'd buy it."

"What he won't buy is rotten meat. You can't bleed it after rigor has set in."

"I just told Big Shoulders to hang it, not bleed it," answered Kip. "If some predator hasn't eaten it by morning, we'll hide it and say a Redpanther dragged it off."

"So can I assume you won't have any problems keeping us supplied with meat?"

"Not with these Orange-Eyes of Kenny's," responded Kip. "I'll swear they could track a billiard ball down three miles of concrete highway."

"So why did you kill two brownbucks then?"

"Because sooner or later Markham's going to want to go hunting Redpanthers or Hooktooths, and I sure don't want him coming out with *me*—so why not bait them right here in camp? It's safer to blow them away from a hide, anyway." He grinned again. "Who knows? Maybe we'll get lucky, and some Redpanther will eat him and we can all go home."

"I wouldn't count on it, Mr. Ngami," said Markham's familiar voice, and we turned to see him standing about twenty yards away from us.

"How long have you been there?" I asked, trying desperately to remember what we had said about him.

"Just for a moment," he said. "I was on my way to see if Mr. Kerr got any worthwhile footage today, though I suppose Mr. Ngami can tell me."

"Not a thing."

"Pity," said Markham, going back to his tent.

"Did he hear me say that I'd shot them at noon?" whispered Kip.

"I don't think so," I replied. "But won't Kerr tell him?"

"It was Kerr's idea to pretend we didn't shoot them until late in the day," said Kip. "He's willing to get rich off Markham, but he doesn't like being in that bastard's company any better than you or I do."

"We talked a lot today," I said. "I suppose he's not so bad, once you understand him."

"Hell, you'd probably sympathize with the Redpanther who's ripping your innards out once you realized she's got babies to feed."

"Never become a bartender, Kip," I said with a smile. "Sympathizing with other people isn't exactly your long and strong suit."

"It doesn't go with my job description—or yours," he said. "But aren't writers supposed to empathize with everyone, to understand what makes 'em all tick?" He paused meaningfully. "Well, Markham's a writer, and if he's ever felt an ounce of sympathy for anyone besides himself, I'll be surprised."

"Not *besides* himself," I corrected him. "*Including* himself. That's what makes him tolerable."

"I can think of a lot of words for him," said Kip. " 'Tolerable' isn't one that comes to mind."

"He doesn't ask us to do anything he himself won't do," I pointed out.

"Sure he does."

"Like what?"

"He asks us to take orders."

"That's not the same thing," I replied. "This is his expedition. He's paying the bills, so he has a right to give the orders."

"If they're stupid orders, do you have a right to disobey them?" asked Kip.

"Of course I do."

He looked at me seriously. "I hope you'll remember that in time of need."

"Are you anticipating any times of need?" I asked, trying to make light of it.

"Plenty of 'em."

15

The next five days were uneventful. We got up each morning, foot-slogged through the mud, and met up with Kip and his team at the end of each day.

On the morning of the sixth day, the rain seemed somewhat lighter, and by midafternoon it had become little more than a drizzle.

"I thought the long rains lasted a couple of months," remarked Markham. "I can see the sun trying to break through that cloud cover."

"They came early, which is an aberration," I said. "Maybe stopping soon is part of the same aberration."

"Let's hope so," he answered. "It'd be nice to finally be able to make some progress. We're barely doing fifteen miles a day now. I see no reason why we can't triple that once the ground dries out."

And sure enough, the rains *did* end that night. Maybe a meteorologist could explain why. Nobody else cared about why; we were just pleased that it was over.

The next morning, as we were preparing to leave, I noticed that Stone Jaw, one of our biggest Orange-Eyes, was having trouble balancing his pack, so I walked over and helped him adjust the weight.

When I returned to Markham, he was pissed as all hell.

"Just what do you think you're doing, Mr. Stone?" he demanded.

"What are you talking about?"

"That Orange-Eye."

"Stone Jaw? What about him?"

"I saw you helping him."

"He was having problems with his pack."

"That's not your concern," he said. "In the future, let Big Shoulders or one of the other Orange-Eyes help him should a similar situation develop."

"It's not a 'situation,' " I said. "It's just an Orange-Eye whose pack was about to slip off."

Markham frowned. "We speak to Big Shoulders because he's the headman, and we occasionally have to speak to Cotton Jacket, because he's the only other Orange-Eye who speaks Terran. But as for the rest, we must keep our distance. Never forget that they're savages, and they greatly outnumber us."

"What kind of bullshit is this?" I shot back. "I seem to remember that three of those 'savages' gave their lives fighting on your behalf."

"Only because they were too stupid to think things through," said Markham. "Put yourself in a similar situation. Would you risk your life fighting against your fellow Men in the service of an Orange-Eye?"

I stared at him without answering.

"Well?" he insisted.

"It's not the same thing."

"It's precisely the same thing."

"All right," I said. "I probably wouldn't kill a Man to protect an Orange-Eye."

"I know that."

"But what does that have to do with helping one of them adjust his load?"

"That makes you his equal and his companion, and you are neither. You are his superior and his leader."

"It seems to me that you're making a lot of fuss over an act of courtesy."

"You perform acts of courtesy to Men, not to dumb animals," answered Markham.

"The Orange-Eyes are a lot of things good and bad," I said, "but dumb animals isn't one of them."

"If it ever comes to a choice, we'll sacrifice every last one of them to save any Man in the party. You're a fool if you *don't* think of them as dumb animals."

Suddenly I noticed Cotton Jacket standing about fifteen yards away, staring intently at us.

"Shut up," I said softly.

"What?" he demanded.

"Be quiet."

He was clearheaded enough to ask why, rather than just shout over me.

"Cotton Jacket."

He looked around. "Where?"

I turned to the Orange-Eye, but he was gone. "He was standing right there, listening to every word you said."

"He probably didn't understand half of it."

"If he understood the other half," I replied, "that could be enough."

"You're crediting him with more brains than he's got," said Markham.

"I hope you're right," I said. "But . . ."

"But what?"

"But I didn't like the expression on his face."

"What expression?" said Markham with a contemptuous snort. "They all look alike all the time."

I kept looking for Cotton Jacket, and finally I spotted him, a quarter of a mile away, speaking animatedly to a number of Orange-Eyes.

"Anyway, you'll remember our little chat, won't you, Mr. Stone?"

"I'll remember it," I said, which was, in my mind at least, different from saying that I would abide by his orders the next time Stone Jaw's pack needed adjusting.

As it turned out, my intentions made no difference.

16

I awoke to Markham grabbing my shoulder and shaking me vigorously.

"Get up, goddammit!" he bellowed.

"What is it?" I asked groggily.

"Your fucking Orange-Eyes have deserted!"

I sat up abruptly. "What are you talking about?"

"Cotton Jacket and Stone Jaw and about two-thirds of them hightailed it out of here during the middle of the night!"

"Did anyone see them?" I asked, still trying to clear my head.

"If I'd seen them, I'd have shot them! Of course nobody saw them!"

I got to my feet and looked out the doorway of my bubble. Big Shoulders was there, and a few others, but the camp looked awfully empty.

"Shit!" I muttered.

"I blame you for this, Mr. Stone," said Markham.

"Me?" I said. *You're* the one he overheard, saying that he

was nothing but an animal and that you'd sacrifice every one of them to save a single Man."

"I only said it because you were foolish enough to mingle with them, and I had to point out your error to you."

"You've got a hell of a funny definition of 'mingle,' " I said.

"We have decisions to make," said Markham, walking out of the bubble. "Honor us with your presence when you're finally awake," he added disgustedly.

I walked to the bathroom, ran the hair atomizer over my face, took a Dryshower, urinated in the Black Hole—no, it wasn't a real black hole, but that's what we called them, since nothing that entered them ever emerged again—and began getting dressed. The thermometer said it was 29 degrees Celsius, and the barometer told me that the rains were indeed over, so after I donned my shirt and shorts, I left my boots under my cot for the bubble boy to put away and just slipped into my sandals.

I walked over to the campfire in front of the mess tent. Markham was waiting there, flanked by all the other men: Kip, Rashid, Kerr, and Arnaz.

"Welcome to the land of the living," said Markham sarcastically.

"Notice any improvement?" added Kip with a grin.

"So what's the situation?" I asked.

"At least they didn't take anything with them," said Markham. "We'll have to go through everything, redistribute what we're keeping, and slow our pace."

"Why slow our pace?"

"Because the Orange-Eyes will be carrying double loads," he answered.

"That's a hell of a way to reward them for being loyal," I said.

"It will just be until we can pick up some more porters," said Markham. "I've already instructed Big Shoulders to tell them we'll pay them double for the whole trip, even though we should come to a village in the next few days."

"How about your team, Kip?" I asked.

"The trackers are all still here."

"And the Dabihs?"

"This isn't their world," answered Kip. "They haven't any place to desert *to.*"

"I've got a question," said Kerr. "Can we count on the remaining Orange-Eyes *not* to desert?"

"Who knows?" I replied with a shrug.

"*You're* supposed to know!" snapped Markham.

"Well, then," I said, "I suppose it all depends on what you say and who overhears you. That is, after all, what precipitated *this* desertion."

"You tell them that the next time one of them deserts, I'll personally hunt him down and shoot him," said Markham.

"If I tell them that, they just might laugh themselves to death," I said. "You're not Kenny Vaughn. If you go out after them in the bush, you'll be hopelessly lost in half an hour."

"This isn't getting us anywhere," said Kip.

"Says the voice of reason," muttered Markham.

"Just trying to help," said Kip. "If you want to call it quits, I'm thrilled."

"No one's calling it quits!" snapped Markham. "Michael Drake is out there somewhere, and I'm going to find him and bring him back, even if I have to do it alone!"

"All right," I said. "Then it's time to get organized. Kip, have Big Shoulders ask your trackers if they'll be willing to carry loads until we can pick up some porters. I haven't spoken to the Dabihs, but I'm sure they don't speak the local dialect, so they must speak some Terran. Ask them if they'll tote some loads too."

"You don't *ask* them," interrupted Markham irritably. "You *tell* them."

"If you want to eat any more meat before the expedition is over, you *ask* them," I corrected him.

He was about to yell at me, but then he considered what I had said and merely nodded to Kip, who went off to find Big Shoulders and the Dabihs.

"You, gentlemen," he continued, turning to Arnaz and Kerr, "will carry your own camera equipment."

"We can't carry it all," protested Kerr. "There's too much of it."

"Then carry what you can, and you can each have one Orange-Eye. Anything you and they can't carry gets left behind." He turned to Rashid. "And you, Doctor, will carry all your medical equipment."

Rashid nodded. "I must point out, Mr. Markham, that Mr. Arnaz is in no condition to carry anything."

"He looks healthy enough to me."

"He has a very serious fungal infection on his torso and shoulders. Any weight pressing against the lesions will be incredibly painful."

Markham stared at Arnaz, as if trying to see through his shirt and determine the true extent of his disability. Finally he shrugged. "All right. Carry what you can in your hands, and you can have an extra Orange-Eye."

We began doping out what we absolutely had to take—clothes, bubbles, mess equipment, the radio, all the other things we tended to take for granted—and decided that we could leave almost half the packs behind, which meant the remaining Orange-Eyes' loads wouldn't be quite double.

Kip rejoined us just as we were finishing, to report that the Dabihs would carry loads, but that his Orange-Eye trackers refused.

"It's a matter of status," he explained. "If you've ever watched them in camp, they don't eat with the rest of the Orange-Eyes, and they hardly ever speak to them. Carrying loads puts you on the lowest rung of the expedition's social ladder, and they feel it's beneath their station."

"We need *every* goddamned Orange-Eye, damn it!" snapped Markham.

"You heard what Enoch said," replied Kip. "Force them to carry loads, and you can forget about eating meat."

"There might be a way," Rashid said slowly.

"What is it?" asked Markham, ready to grasp at any straw.

"I won't guarantee they'll go for it," said Rashid. "But if it's a matter of status, what if we gave them the biggest loads? Not necessarily the heaviest, but the bulkiest—so they could look like they're carrying three times as much as the other Orange-Eyes. Would that increase their status . . . or would it just make them look like suckers?"

"We'll never know until we ask," I said, getting up and walking over to Big Shoulders. At first he was offended, since we were trying to make "his" Orange-Eyes look bad to please Kenny's Orange-Eyes . . . but when I explained that we were actually tricking those snobbish, superior trackers into carrying loads, he agreed to put the question to them. They talked back and forth for almost ten minutes, but finally Big Shoulders returned and reported that they had agreed to our little subterfuge.

We repacked all the equipment, broke down the camp, and set off to the south and east. I couldn't help feeling that, despite all his anger and bluster, Markham was secretly delighted, since the desertion gave him a few more articles and would help assure his immortality should he overcome these suddenly greater odds against simply surviving, let alone finding Michael Drake.

17

As the ground dried out and became hard, we made much better progress. Because the loads were heavier, we didn't do the fifty or sixty miles a day Markham had hoped for, but we managed about thirty-five, which was a good five hundred percent better than we'd been doing before the rains stopped.

I suggested that now might be a good time to ask someone in Fort Capstick to fly out with some supplies and new vehicles, but Markham rejected the notion. The terrain was so uneven, so filled with hidden rocks and holes, so devoid of any discernible trail to follow, that we would do better on foot.

He did contact Fort Capstick, however, to see if Stuart had been rescued yet. The answer was pretty much what Cotton Jacket had predicted. They were sure we'd given them the wrong coordinates, because when they landed the members of the village swore they'd never seen Stuart or us. There was no way to prove otherwise, and after a brief, unsuccessful search for the injured pilot, the rescue crew had no choice but to return home empty-handed. Markham never mentioned Stuart again; I'd like to think it was from guilt, but more likely it was just lack of interest.

We entered an uncharted territory—hell, two-thirds of the planet was uncharted—and I noticed that the landscape began changing once again. We began following a major river, and since it didn't exist on the map, Markham decided to call it the Markham River. (If you buy a map of the planet today, you'll find that became its official name.)

The river ran through a forest, and we stumbled upon some flowering trees I had never seen before. They were perhaps seventy-five feet tall, with brilliant red and gold blossoms. The lower branches also produced a succulent berry, which Rashid analyzed as best he could and finally decided that it could be eaten with no ill effects. I was the first to try one, and it was as sweet a fruit as I'd ever tasted.

The forest was alive with animals and insects. There were dozens of primate species living in the upper terraces of the trees, and before long we were able to identify two new predators, both catlike, one spotted, one striped, both able to climb trees with remarkable agility.

I shot a new species of herbivore one day as it edged too close to our camp. Markham explained that that gave me the right to name it. I declined, and a moment later, with his foot on the neck of the carcass and Arnaz's holo camera trained on him, he explained to his audience that this was a Markham's Wild-buck.

"I never saw anyone so determined to name so many things after himself," muttered Kip disgustedly, as Markham continued speaking into the camera.

"Immortality," I said.

"What?"

"Nothing."

"Anyway, it's a damned good thing we already have a name for the Orange-Eyes, or he'd be telling everyone that we decided to call them Markhams."

"Naming places and objects is the right of the discoverer," I said with a shrug.

"You think he's the first guy ever to see one of those trees, or this animal?" said Kip. "He's probably not even the first to name them." He grimaced. "He's just the first to do it for a news camera."

"That presents an interesting philosophical question," I said with a smile. "If you name an animal in an empty forest, does anyone hear you?"

He grimaced. "Only if your name's Markham."

"Well, cheer up," I said. "He can only name one river and one herbivore after himself."

"Want to bet?" Kip shot back. "Before long we'll have a Lake Markham, a Markham Ocean, a Markham Falls, and God knows how many species of Markham animals."

"Then we'll learn to live with it," I said.

"Not me," said Kip. "I'm going to name every new animal and bush and flower I see after myself, just so he can't slap his own name onto everything."

"Whatever makes you happy," I said, trying to end the conversation.

"Hey, look what I've got!" said a voice from behind us, and we turned to see Kerr walking toward us with a coal-black avian perched on his forearm.

"What the hell is *that?*" asked Kip.

"I don't know. It's black and it's got wings." Kerr looked up and smiled. "Crooked Leg was about to kill it. He'd killed its mother and all of its siblings in their nest. I guess the Orange-Eyes eat these things."

"So you rescued it?" I asked.

"Right. I'm going to name it Edgar."

"Why Edgar?" asked Kip.

"For Edgar Allan Poe," said Kerr.

"Never heard of him."

"He wrote a poem about a raven, back when we were still Earthbound," explained Kerr. "I read it in college, and it's stayed with me."

"What do you feed it?"

"I don't know," said Kerr. "I pull dozens of insects out of my hair every day. I'll see if it wants them. And we can try some of those berries that we've all been eating."

"Yeah, one or the other ought to work," I said. "I mean, hell, this is where it lives, so it figures to eat whatever we find around here."

Kerr stroked the avian's neck gently. It flinched at first, then leaned forward so he could do it again.

"Maybe I'll even talk the boss into doing a feature on it." He smiled. "Imagine! *My* ugly face showing up in five billion homes."

"He's reaching that many people?" I asked, surprised.

Kerr nodded. "Maybe even more. According to the subspace radio, the whole damned Democracy is sitting on pins and needles, waiting for him to find Michael Drake. They're gobbling up his daily reports like candy."

"And what happens if Drake is dead, or on some other world?" I continued.

"I don't think Markham's given it two seconds' thought," replied Kerr. "And to tell the truth, neither have I. We've got a hot story here. We'll stick with it until it's played out one way or the other."

"One way or the other?" repeated Kip, puzzled.

"Until we find him, or everyone gets bored with our looking for him," answered Kerr. "Don't forget—this is more than a story about finding a lost man. This particular man may have the cure for ybonia."

He walked off, cooing at Edgar, which cooed back, and I turned to Kip.

"Even if he's alive, which I doubt," I began, "even if he's around the next bend in the trail, which I further doubt, I can't believe he's found a cure for ybonia. How the hell could you discover something like that and keep it secret? Especially a man like Drake. He'd have reported it the day he found it, and probably given the formula away for free."

"No one could live out here all these years," added Kip. "Look at Kenny. He knew the Orange-Eyes better than anyone, and they killed him anyway."

"That's not entirely fair," I said. "It was Markham who precipitated the attack."

"And if Michael Drake is here," continued Kip, "it's because he *wants* to be here, and he may go to war if Markham tries to bring him back to the Democracy against his will."

Markham finally finished speaking into the camera and ordered the Orange-Eyes to skin and bleed the carcass, then wandered over to join us.

"I hope that thing tastes better than it looks," he said. "Still, it made a nice story. That's one hell of a sharp set of horns on that beast. You get the feeling they could pierce a granite boulder."

"All he wanted to do was get away," I said. "Besides, I don't think those horns are for defense. I've got a feeling they're strictly for fighting other males for breeding rights to the females."

"That's because you have no imagination," said Markham. "Tell Big Shoulders to save the horns for me."

"As a trophy?"

"I shoot my own trophies," replied Markham. "No, what I want to do is get a feature. I'll attach a horn to a long, straight pole and show how the wags use it to hunt meat."

"But they don't."

"For all you know, they do," he shot back. "Besides, it makes a good story, and who does it hurt?"

"Only thing it hurts is your credibility," said Kip.

"Let someone come out here and live with every goddamned tribe of Orange-Eyes on the planet to prove me wrong," said Markham. "In the meantime, I've got another feature—and if they *don't* use the horns for spears, maybe some of our wags will watch me and start using them."

"I think they'd rather use your Burner or your Screecher," I said.

"That's not a bad idea," replied Markham, suddenly excited.

"What's not?" I asked, confused.

"Tell Big Shoulders to pass the word: I'll give the first wag to spot Michael Drake a choice between my Screecher or my Burner." He paused. "Hell, I'll go tell him myself. I *like* that idea, Mr. Stone!"

As he walked away, Kip turned to me and said, in a voice low enough that only I could hear it, "Didn't Ahab nail a gold piece to the mast of the *Pequod* as a reward for the first man to spot the White Whale?"

"He was looking for a monster that killed men; we're looking for a saint who saves them."

"You're talking about the prey," said Kip. "I'm talking about the captain."

18

We spent another week traveling through the riverine forest with no sign of habitation, and nothing remotely resembling a trail that could accommodate vehicles, even if there was a way to transport some here from Fort Capstick.

It had been getting warmer each day, and even though the rains seemed to be over, the air was thick and humid. Finally I got tired of taking chemical Dryshowers and decided to take a dip in the river.

"Not smart," said Kip, when I announced my intentions during breakfast. "You don't know what the hell is swimming around in there."

"I haven't seen anything that looks dangerous," I said. "Nothing with teeth, nothing with claws."

"It's what you *don't* see that gets you."

"I'll beat the water with a stick to scare everything away," I told him.

"For all you know, beating the water with a stick is like saying 'Come and get it!' to whatever's hungry."

"Then come along and ride shotgun."

"If I shoot the water with a laser, I could scald you to death, and I don't know what effect a Screecher has when you aim it into the water."

"He's a grown man," said Markham, speaking up at last. "If he wants to take a dip, it's his decision."

"Can you afford to lose him?" asked Kip.

"I haven't seen anything dangerous in any body of water on this planet," answered Markham.

"You didn't answer my question," persisted Kip.

"We're not losing anyone," snapped Markham. Then he paused. "But just in case . . ." He looked over to the cameramen, who were eating a few yards away. "Mr. Kerr, go down to the river with Mr. Stone and tape him while he bathes."

"Great idea," said Kerr sardonically. "Very commercial. I'm sure we can sell bootlegs to spinster ladies all across the galaxy."

"If nothing happens, wipe the holotape."

"What might happen?"

"Who knows?" replied Markham. "If he gets eaten, I want it captured for posterity."

"What if he's only partially eaten, and manages to drag himself to safety on the bank, missing maybe only a leg and his genitals?" asked Arnaz with a smile.

"Then we'll toss you into the river to hunt for them," said Markham irritably. "I don't need a humorist this early in the day."

"Why don't you just take a Dryshower and make everybody happy?" urged Kip.

"I'm sick of Dryshowers," I said stubbornly. "I want to feel real water on my body."

"It's not as if it's going to get you clean," said Kip. "Look at how muddy the water is, and all the fish and animals that are shitting in it." He paused. "Hell, you'll probably need a Dryshower when you're done."

"I don't care," I said. "I grew up with water, and I miss it. I've been taking Dryshowers every day since we got here." I paused. "Besides, I swam the last time I was on Bushveld, and nothing happened to me."

"Maybe your number's up this time."

"I'll leave you two to fight it out," said Markham, getting up and heading off toward his bubble. "I've got some writing to do."

"Why the hell are you making such a fuss about this?" I asked Kip after Markham had left.

"If you get eaten, I'm going to have to spend that much more time with him," he replied with a guilty grin.

"Now I understand your concern, you bastard," I said wryly. "Hell, I almost hope I *do* get eaten, just so you have to eat every meal in his company."

"Some friend."

"You took the words right out of my mouth."

After I finished my breakfast I went to my bubble, slipped out of my clothes, wrapped a towel around my waist, and, carrying another over my shoulder, I walked to Kerr's bubble.

"You ready?" I asked.

"Yeah, just putting Edgar in a cage I had one of the Orange-Eyes build," he said, emerging a moment later with a small holo camera and a sidearm.

"I never saw you carry a weapon before," I remarked.

"Our esteemed employer's wishes to the contrary, I'd rather save your life than record its tragic conclusion," he answered, patting the butt of the gun. Suddenly he smiled. "That's probably why I'll never be as rich or famous as he is."

"Trust me," I said. "Nothing's going to bother me. If you don't have a secret yen to watch a naked man swimming in an alien river, you're in for a boring ten minutes."

"I hope so," he said.

We walked a couple of hundred yards to the riverbank. The current was moderate, and it was only about forty yards wide at that point. The water was a murky brown, and here and there I could see an alien fish break the surface as it tried to catch an insect that was resting on top of the water.

I looked around, found a large branch that had fallen off a tree recently enough to still be green, and picked it up. Then I walked in up to my knees and began beating the water with the branch. I kept it up for about twenty seconds while Kerr fiddled nervously with his gun, then threw the branch back to shore, stepped out until the water was waist-high, and slowly lowered myself until I was totally submerged.

It felt wonderful, and I realized just how much I had missed bathing in water rather than a spray of dry chemicals. I broke the surface, walked to the middle of the river, which was barely up to my neck, and began swimming against the current.

"Careful!" shouted Kerr. "You don't know what's coming this way!"

If it had been Markham I'd have ignored him, but I liked Kerr, so I let the current slowly bring me back until I was opposite him. Then I stopped and just stood there, luxuriating in the feel of the water rushing past my body.

A small fish swam up and began nibbling, tentatively and toothlessly, on my leg. I reached down, grabbed it, and threw it ashore.

"That's your reward for watching me!" I yelled. "Fresh fish for lunch!"

Kerr picked up the flopping fish and threw it back into the river.

"No, thanks!" he called back. "The Orange-Eyes don't eat fish, and if they don't like them, Lord knows what they would do to a Man's metabolism."

"I've had them before," I said. "They're good. Hardly any fishy taste at all. If you cook it right, it tastes kind of like chicken—or if you've ever been to Karimon out on the Spiral Arm, like a young Fleetjumper."

"I'll pass on it anyway."

"Your loss," I said.

"You feel clean enough and wet enough yet?" he asked after a few more minutes had passed.

"Yeah," I said, unhappy at the thought of getting back on dry land. "I'm coming."

I started walking back to where I'd left my towels, just a few yards from where Kerr was standing, but suddenly I stepped on something sharp—a shell, a rock, I don't know what it was. I yelped, grabbed my foot, lost my balance, submerged for a moment, and started floating downstream.

Kerr pulled his gun out and began pacing me on the bank, looking for something to shoot. "Where is it?" he shouted. "What's got hold of you?"

"There's nothing here!" I managed to yell. "I just stepped on something sharp."

"Are you bleeding?"

"Probably."

"You'd better get out fast," he said anxiously. "Who knows what the hell the smell of blood will attract. Can you walk on it?"

"Yeah, I was just startled," I said, righting myself and half-walking, half-swimming to the shore.

Which was when I saw it.

It was beautifully camouflaged. At first it appeared to be nothing but some weeds sticking up out of the shallows. Even when I got closer, I would never have spotted it except for the swirling water, which was caused by the struggling fish.

I walked right up to it, squatted down on my haunches, and stared at it.

"What have you got there?" asked Kerr, coming over.

"Take a look," I said.

He studied it for a moment. "It's a fish trap," he said at last.

"That's right."

"Very primitive."

"And very effective," I said, pointing to half a dozen fish that were struggling fruitlessly to escape from the woven net of weeds.

Kerr frowned. "But the Orange-Eyes don't eat fish."

"At least *our* Orange-Eyes don't," I agreed.

"I don't think any of them do. Big Shoulders told me fish make them sick. I mean, if it was against their religion, well, religions change from one location to another. But metabolisms don't. If fish make *our* Orange-Eyes sick, they must make *all* Orange-Eyes sick."

"That's what's so interesting," I said. "Who else do you know who can make a fish trap?"

"A Man can."

"My thinking exactly." I paused. "Can you think of any Men who might have come this way ahead of us?"

"Jesus!" said Kerr. "We're closer to Michael Drake than we thought!"

"I know," I said. "And consider this: None of the fish were dead. That means someone's been by to empty this trap in the last couple of days." I stepped onto the bank, picked up a towel, and started to dry myself off. "Well, let's go tell Markham the good news."

"You know," said Kerr as we walked back to camp, "he's the most famous man in the Democracy, and he's been missing and presumed dead for fifteen years. And now we're within a day or two of finding him."

"Right."

"I don't know."

"What's wrong?" I asked.

"A little voice keeps telling me that it can't be this easy."

19

Markham was ecstatic over the news, and we broke the camp in record time. There were no trails to follow, so we just kept walking alongside the river. I had Big Shoulders order Kip's trackers to fan out ahead of us, looking for signs of Michael Drake.

We found two more fish traps in the next three miles, again with every indication that they'd been emptied out within the past day or two.

Markham kept muttering to himself, and finally I asked him if something was wrong.

"No, everything's right," he said excitedly. "I'm just trying out different opening lines, since the whole thing is going to be captured for posterity. I'm trying to get a feel for which will play better."

"Why not just say hello?" I asked.

"That's hardly a greeting to endear you to ten billion people," said Markham contemptuously. "I haven't quite hit on the words, but when I do, they'll be something unique, so that whenever they're repeated people will always identify them with me."

My inclination was to suggest that he say, "Hello, Mike, you old bastard. Where the hell have you been hiding yourself for the past fifteen years?," but somehow I thought the humor would be lost on him, so I just kept on walking, gradually slowing my pace so that before long I found myself walking side by side with Kip, a good forty yards behind Markham.

"So we're really going to find him?" asked Kip. "I was starting to think we were just going to walk once around the planet and then go home."

"Unless some other Man went out into the bush and never came back, it's got to be him," I said. "And I'm not aware of anyone else who's missing."

"I wonder if he's in any condition to walk back?"

"If he isn't, I suppose that we can clear an area for a plane to land," I said. "One that can take him and Markham back, anyway."

"What about the rest of us?"

"It can always return for us. The main thing is to get Michael Drake back to civilization."

"Well, it looks like this expedition should be over in a couple of days," said Kip. "It's a damned good thing I didn't talk you out of taking that swim."

"You sure tried hard enough."

"Well, like I told you, I—" Suddenly he stared ahead of us. "What's the matter now?"

Markham had come to a stop and was staring intently at something on the ground. Kip and I hurried forward to join him.

"What's *that*, Mr. Stone?" asked Markham, pointing to the ground.

I looked down. It was a track unlike anything I had seen before.

"Beats me," I said. "It's not hooved, and it's obviously not one of the big catlike carnivores."

"No toes," remarked Kip.

"I don't need to know what it *isn't*," said Markham. "I want to know what it *is*."

"I never saw anything like it," I said. "It's got pads, like a cat, but no claws."

"What about retractable claws?"

"They don't have them, not on Bushveld."

I brushed some fallen leaves aside.

"What are you looking for?" asked Markham.

"More prints. We can't tell from this if it's two-legged, four-legged, or some other combination."

"I don't care about that," said Markham. "All I want to know is: Is it dangerous? We haven't got much visibility in this damned forest. If this is something that can attack us, I need to know what we're facing."

"All I can tell you is that it's not going to rip you asunder with the foot that made that print," I said. "Maybe Kenny could have identified it; *I* can't."

"But you were on Bushveld before."

"Doesn't mean a thing," I replied. "Pick any planet you want, and if it doesn't have a zoo, you could wander across it for twenty years without seeing even half of its animal species."

Markham sighed. "Point taken." He could be a son of a bitch and a martinet, but I'll grant him this: In all the time I knew him, he never tried to stare a fact down.

We spent a couple of minutes looking for more tracks, but we couldn't find any. They may have been there to begin with, but by the time we cleared away all the leaves and other debris, we'd cleared away any tracks as well. I found myself wishing, for perhaps the hundredth time, that Kenny was still with us; not for his friendship, which I also missed, but for his knowledge of the bush. *He'd* have known how to move leaves and sticks without harming the tracks. I didn't.

We were about to continue on when one of the trackers came up to us, accompanied by a Dabih. The tracker babbled excitedly in his own dialect. I understood a few words, but since the Dabih spoke Terran, I turned to him and asked him to explain what they'd seen.

"There is a village about a kilometer distant, to the south and east," said the Dabih. "But it is not inhabited by Orange-Eyes."

"By Men?" I asked, wondering if Drake had taken some assistants with him.

"No," said the Dabih.

"By who, then?" demanded Markham.

The Dabih shrugged, sending muscular ripples down the length of his plum-colored body. "Strange creatures," he said. "I do not recognize them."

"Did the tracker?"

"No. They are entirely unknown to him."

I pointed to the track we'd found. "Could one of them have made this?"

"Yes."

"What do they look like?" I asked.

"My Terran is limited," said the Dabih. "Better that you see for yourself."

"Your Terran seems fine," said Markham.

He shook his head. "Truly, I do not have the words for it," he said.

"Did they see you?" I asked.

"No."

"What is their village like?"

"Mud dwellings, hardened by the sun. They layer large leaves for the roofs."

"Well, they live in huts and they know how to make fish traps," said Kip. "They're obviously intelligent."

"They're obviously *sentient*," Markham corrected him. "How intelligent they are remains to be seen." He paused. "I just hope they're advanced enough to have a barter economy."

"Why?"

"Because we need porters. I'm going to have to hire some, or else buy them from the headman."

"Maybe we should wait to see what they look like," I suggested. "They might be incapable of carrying our loads."

"If they can carry fish from the river to their village, they can carry loads," said Markham decisively.

"Perhaps they're intelligent enough not to want to," suggested Kip.

Markham glared at him contemptuously for a moment, but made no reply.

"Well, so much for meeting Michael Drake today," I said.

"This is very disappointing," agreed Markham. "I could have sworn those fish traps . . ." He shrugged. "Oh, well, we wouldn't want to find him too easily, would we?"

"Too easily?" repeated Kip. "We lost our plane and our vehicles, Kenny Vaughn's dead, the pilot is probably dead, we've been attacked by Orange-Eyes, half our porters have deserted, we don't know for sure if Drake's even on Bushveld alive *or* dead, and you're worried that we might find him too easily?"

Markham turned slowly and stared at Kip. "You are starting to annoy me, Mr. Ngami," he said coldly.

There was something about the way he said it that convinced Kip to keep his mouth shut.

"Well, Mr. Stone," said Markham, "let's go meet this new species. If nothing else, we should get some interesting features to send back to the Democracy." He paused. "Mr. Arnaz, Mr. Kerr, have your cameras at the ready." Finally he turned to the Dabih. "Lead the way, please."

The Dabih, his purple chest puffed out with self-importance, strode forward, and we all fell into step behind him. After about a quarter mile he turned inland from the river, and the forest started to thin out.

Finally we came to a clearing, and we could see the village perhaps a hundred yards ahead.

"It certainly doesn't resemble an Orange-Eye village, does it?" remarked Markham. "There's no geometrical pattern to it, and the huts are much more primitive. See? One small doorway, a tiny hole in the roof for smoke to exit, and nothing else. And while they *seem* round, they're actually irregular."

"No boreholes, either," I noted. "That means they drink from the river."

"You bathed in it."

"Bathing's one thing," I replied. "I'd never drink it unless it was purified."

"They've probably been doing it for millennia," said Markham. "They've doubtless adapted to the point where all the germs and impurities actually have a beneficial effect."

"Here comes one!" whispered Kip excitedly.

Emerging into the clearing from another part of the forest was one of the village's inhabitants. It was a female, carrying an infant in a grass sling that hung down from her neck.

She walked upright, but her legs were short and slightly bowed, as if her very recent ancestors had lived in trees and had only recently decided to start dwelling on the ground. Her arms were not long like an ape's, but rather of normal size and lightly muscled, very much like a woman's. Her hands had long, lean fingers and opposable thumbs.

But it was her skin that drew my immediate attention. It was scaly, not moist like a reptile's, but dry and crusty, looking almost like she had some disfiguring disease. There were regular eruptions, sharp points that stuck out at odd angles, furthering the illusion of a serious skin condition.

Her face was not frightening, but it wasn't comforting, either. Her teeth were yellow, her nostrils were two barely discernible slits, her eyes red—not bloodshot, though that was the impression one got—and her scalp was covered by thin tufts of hair, as if she were in the process of going bald.

As horrible an impression as she made, I noticed that she walked with a healthy spring to her stride, and the added weight of the infant she was carrying didn't seem to impede her in any way.

"Boy, talk about plug-ugly!" whispered Kip.

"Indeed," replied Markham. "I don't think I've ever seen anything quite so repellent." Suddenly he turned to Kip. "That's a good name for them, Mr. Ngami."

"I don't know what you're talking about," said Kip, confused.

"Plug-Uglies," answered Markham. "We'll come up with an official name later, but for our own use, I think that will suffice."

"I'd hold off on that," I interjected. "For all you know, she's got a serious case of eczema or the equivalent, and none of the others looks like that."

"The hell they don't," said Markham, looking ahead.

Half a dozen other females had emerged from their huts to greet the one we had seen, and all bore the same lesions and eruptions on their bodies.

"Why would God make anybody look like that?" mused Kip.

"I'm sure there are sound biological reasons," said Markham.

"Such as?"

"We'll never learn observing them from afar," said Markham. "Let's go introduce ourselves. Mr. Stone, how's your sign language?"

"Probably about the same as yours," I said.

"That bad?" said Markham with a smile. "Well, we'll just have to make do."

And, with that, he stepped out of the forest and began walking toward the village. Kip and I followed him, and then the cameramen joined us, and finally the Dabihs and Orange-Eyes fell into step.

A tall male Plug-Ugly, even more dreadful in appearance than the females, stepped out of a hut in the center of the village and began approaching us.

"How would you signal that we come in peace?" whispered Markham.

"I'd throw down our weapons," I answered.

"Use your brain, Mr. Stone," said Markham. "They've never seen a Man before. They don't *know* that these things are weapons." He paused. "Should I raise a hand, or bow, or—?"

Suddenly our problems were solved for us, as the Plug-Ugly stopped directly in front of us.

"Welcome," he said in a deep, guttural voice. "We are most happy to greet you. If you are hungry, we shall prepare a feast for you."

"Thank you very much," replied Markham, just before it dawned on him, and all the rest of us, that we had been addressed *in Terran*.

20

We are very happy to receive such a cordial welcome," said Markham.

"We have only the friendliest of feelings toward members of your race," said the Plug-Ugly.

Did you notice that? He's seen Men before!

"My name is Robert Markham. By what name or title shall I address you?"

"I am Ponta." He extended his scaly hand. "I am pleased to meet you, Robert Markham."

Ask him where he learned the language, I wanted to scream at him, but Markham, who was probably even more eager to know the answer than I was, ignored the subject.

"We have not met any members of your race before," he said. "What do you call yourselves?"

"We are the People."

"And in your own language?"

The Plug-Ugly's lips drew back in what I assumed was a smile. "You could not pronounce it, Robert Markham."

"Are you native to this world?" continued Markham.

"Certainly."

"I wonder why your existence has remained unknown?"

"It is known to *us*," said Ponta.

"How many of you are there?"

"In this village?"

"On the whole world," said Markham.

"I have no idea," answered Ponta. "Many."

Markham pulled out a smokeless cigar, rolled it between his thumb and forefinger as he studied it, and finally lit it.

"The man who taught you my language—where is he now?"

"You mean Michael Drake?"

A triumphant smile crossed Markham's face. "That's precisely who I mean. Where can I find him?"

"I have no idea."

"How long since he was here?"

"Four"—Ponta searched for the right word and finally found it—"*weeks.*"

"Michael Drake was here four weeks ago?" demanded Markham excitedly.

"Yes. He spent many weeks with us. That is how so many of us came to learn Terran."

"And he's still alive?"

"Certainly," said Ponta. "He has been touched by God. No one can kill him." The Plug-Ugly paused. "That is why we know you and we will become good friends. No member of Michael Drake's race can be evil."

"What did he do while he was here?" asked Markham.

Ponta turned toward the huts and said something in his own language. It sounded like a frog being skewered. A moment later two small children emerged from the nearest hut.

"These are my sons," explained Ponta, signaling them to approach us. "The taller was sickly, and was wasting away. Michael Drake's magic made him well. The smaller one's leg was shredded by a Hooktooth, and he could not walk." Ponta paused. "Look at him now that Michael Drake has cured him. You cannot even tell which leg was injured."

"So he came here and made your sick people well?" said Markham.

"He did many things," answered the Plug-Ugly, as more and more curious faces peeked out from their huts to stare at us. "He taught us Terran, and he explained why we must boil our water and cook our meat and wash our vegetables. And every night he would gather the entire village about him, and he would tell us of the Great Flood, and the Ten Commandments, and the Sermon on the Mount, and the Magna Carta, and the Sirius Statement of Universal Liberties, and the Declaration of Spica II." Suddenly he looked around and raised his voice. "You have nothing to fear!" he called out, still speaking in Terran. "Come out and greet Michael Drake's brothers!"

Slowly, in twos and threes, the rest of the Plug-Uglies emerged from their huts and cautiously approached us. There couldn't have been sixty in all.

"He couldn't have wasted months on a village this small, could he?" whispered Kip.

"Could they have learned Terran any sooner?" I replied.

"I suppose not," admitted Kip. "But why does a man who can save billions of lives bury himself here with sixty aliens for God knows how long . . .?"

"*They* aren't the aliens," I corrected him. "*We* are. This is their world, remember?"

"Don't give me semantics!" snapped Kip softly. "I'm asking a legitimate question. Why would a man as important as Michael Drake spend maybe half a year of his life curing snakebite and teaching the Bible to a bunch of savages?"

"It sounds to me like he cured a lot more than snakebite and he taught a lot more than the Bible," I whispered back.

We turned our attention back to the Plug-Uglies, who had completely surrounded us. Their manner wasn't hostile, or even curious—just polite. Then, as if in response to some unseen signal, they all sat down.

"I have a question," said one female who was nearing maturity.

"I'll do my best to answer it," said Markham. "But then you people will have to answer one for me."

"A trade!" said Ponta happily. "An answer for an answer! Thus will we exchange information. I am sure Michael Drake would have approved!"

"Do you mind if my cameramen take holos of this?" asked Markham.

He tried unsuccessfully to explain what holos *were,* but he at least convinced them that they weren't dangerous, and while Kerr and Arnaz began operating their equipment, he turned back to the female.

"Why did not Jesus kill the Pharisees?" she asked. "Why did he allow himself to be crucified?"

"I'll be damned if I know," admitted Markham. "If it had been me, I'd have wiped out the Pharisees *and* the Romans."

"I believe I can answer that," said Rashid, the only Man in the party who probably didn't have a Christian anywhere in his family tree. He launched into an explanation that satisfied him and mystified everyone else.

When he was done, Markham spoke again.

"An answer for an answer," he reminded them. "Where can I find Michael Drake?"

There was some buzzing back and forth in their own dialect. Then a mature male spoke up. "We cannot give you an exact location, but we know he has gone to the south."

"Why?" asked Markham. "What's south of here that interests him?"

"He is exploring and mapping the area," said Ponta. "He believes he will find an enormous lake to the south."

"So he makes maps, too?"

"Oh, yes," replied Ponta. "When he finally returns to Fort Capstick, he will turn over all his maps and notes to the government there." He offered his equivalent of a smile again. "And now it is our turn to ask a question."

"All right."

"Why do Men make war?"

"Why does anyone?" responded Markham. "Sometimes there are irreconcilable political differences."

"You misunderstand me. I know the *reasons* for war. I know why the People fight wars, and why the Orange-Eyes do. But if all Men are like Michael Drake, if they are all equally touched by God, then why do *they* ever fight wars?"

"I think you answered your own question," said Markham. "All Men are not like Michael Drake. He is very special, even among his own race."

We traded questions back and forth for the next half hour, the Plug-Uglies trying to understand what made lesser Men than Michael Drake tick, Markham trying to pinpoint where Drake was and where he might be going next. Finally Ponta announced that it was time for our banquet, and we all gathered in the very center of the village, Men and Plug-Uglies and Orange-Eyes alike, and sat down to what was, in truth, a rather mediocre meal of cooked vegetables and some unidentifiable meat.

"Will you stay with us?" asked Ponta when the meal was over. "There is much we wish to learn from you."

"I'm afraid we can't," said Markham. "Michael Drake is the one Man who can cure a disease that is decimating our population; it is essential that we find him. We'll be leaving within the hour." He paused. "That brings up another matter. We've lost about half our porters. I should like to borrow some of your people to help us carry our loads."

"I am sorry, but we cannot help you," said Ponta.

"I would pay very well," continued Markham. "Or, if you have no use for credits, I would pay you in meat or salt or any other form of barter."

"The People are not porters, and we do not leave our village except to hunt." Ponta paused. "We mean no insult. We would not do this even for Michael Drake."

"Drake asked and you refused?"

"No. But *if* he had asked, we would have refused."

"That would hardly be a display of friendship, or of gratitude for all the good he did you."

"We know that he would not make us act contrary to our tradition," answered Ponta. "The Orange-Eyes carry loads; the People do not."

"Well, I'm afraid I don't have a choice. I must obtain porters."

"There is a village of Orange-Eyes ten days to the south and east," said Ponta, pointing in its direction. "Probably you can hire porters there."

"I can't wait that long. My Orange-Eyes have been carrying double loads since our vehicles broke down."

"What is a vehicle?"

"Never mind," said Markham. "I will ask you one last time: Will you give me twenty-five porters? We'll send them back as soon as we can obtain more Orange-Eyes."

"I cannot, Robert Markham," said Ponta. "But you are welcome to leave your loads here, and pick them up when you return with Michael Drake."

"We may not be coming back this way."

"You will. Michael Drake now has a map."

Markham got to his feet. "This has gone on long enough. I

have no more time to waste. I must have porters. You will supply them."

"I have already explained—"

"I *will* have them," said Markham ominously, drawing his laser pistol. He looked at the assembled Plug-Uglies and raised his voice so they could all hear him. "I will point to the ones I want to use as porters. When I point to each of you, you will stand up and walk over to where my porters have left their loads." He waved the pistol meaningfully. "Have no doubt about this: I will kill anyone who refuses."

He pointed to a large, broad-shouldered male. "You first."

The Plug-Ugly simply stared at him and refused to move.

Markham didn't threaten, didn't plead, didn't count to three. He just pointed the pistol at the Plug-Ugly and fired. The Plug-Ugly keeled over, a smoking black hole between his eyes.

"Don't try to help him!" snapped Markham, as Plug-Uglies, Orange-Eyes, Dabihs, and Rashid rushed over to him. "He's dead."

The females froze.

"Sit down!"

They sat down.

Markham pointed his pistol at another male. "You."

The male refused to budge, and Markham killed him a moment later, then whirled and aimed his guns at the Plug-Uglies.

"No one moves until I tell him to," he grated, as I grabbed Kip's arm.

"He'll kill them all!" whispered Kip.

"Including you, if you try to stop him," I shot back.

The next Plug-Ugly Markham indicated got up and walked over to the loads, and suddenly, as if they had all been waiting for just one member of the tribe to choose life over tradition, everyone Markham pointed at agreed to become a porter.

Suddenly Markham turned to Kerr.

"You haven't been filming all this, have you?" he demanded furiously.

"You told me to take holos," replied Kerr. "You never told me to stop."

"I'm telling you now. And destroy everything since the end of the meal."

Kerr shrugged. "You're the boss."

Markham turned back to Ponta. "If you're right about the Orange-Eye village to the south, I'll send your people back ten days from now."

"God will punish you severely for what you have done this day," said Ponta.

"God will thank me for finding Michael Drake all the sooner," retorted Markham.

"Michael Drake will know that you have killed two of the People, and he will not come back with you."

"Oh?" said Markham. "And who will tell him?"

"He is Michael Drake," said Ponta. "He will know."

"You are confusing Men with gods."

"And you are confusing a god with a mere Man."

"God or Man, I mean to find him and bring him back to the Democracy," said Markham. He turned to the rest of our party. "It's time to move out. We can still cover a few miles before dark."

Big Shoulders had divided up the loads, and now each of the Plug-Uglies we had forcibly added to our crew lifted a load onto his shoulders, as did all of our Orange-Eye porters. The trackers led the way, unencumbered, followed by the Dabihs, Rashid, Kip, and the cameramen. I was about to join them when I felt a heavy hand on my shoulder.

"You and I will bring up the rear," said Markham.

"They won't attack us," I said. "Look around you. They don't have any weapons."

"Then you have nothing to worry about, do you?" he replied.

"I don't understand why we're doing this," I said, as the last of the Plug-Uglies walked by and we fell into step behind them. "Even you don't think they're going to start throwing sticks and stones at us."

"Of course not—but I don't trust that Ponta. He might try sending a runner to Michael Drake's camp to feed him all kinds of lies about us."

"Why tell him lies?" I said. "From what I know about Drake, he'll find the truth apalling enough."

"I did what I had to do," said Markham. "I apologize to no one."

"We could have just trekked to the Orange-Eye village," I said.

"It would have cost us a few days, and we can't spare them, not now that we're so close to him."

"You make him sound like some animal we're hunting."

"I suppose, in a way, he is," replied Markham thoughtfully.

21

We trekked south for eight days. On two different occasions some of the Plug-Uglies tried to escape and return to their village. Both times Markham had the Dabihs and trackers hunt them down and bring them back. Then he tied their arms to a tree and gave them each ten strokes with his whip. Rashid was forbidden to tend their wounds, and the Dabihs were posted as camp guards each night.

"I've just about had it," muttered Kip one evening as he and I sat alone beside a dying fire. Markham was in his bubble, dictating something or other, and almost all the other members of our four races were sleeping. "A slave caravan can't feel much different from this."

I didn't reply, but just stared unhappily at the glowing embers.

"Well?" demanded Kip.

"Well what?"

"What do you say—why don't we just pack up and start

walking north? We can probably reach the vehicles in three or
four weeks, and hit Fort Capstick a week after that."

"Forget it," I said.

"Why? Surely you don't approve of the way he's treating
these poor bastards!"

"Of course not. But if we leave, he'll only take it out on them.
You know that."

"Then what do you propose to do?"

"Help him find Michael Drake, and the sooner the better,"
I answered him. "Maybe *we* can't control him, but you can bet
your ass Drake won't permit this kind of treatment."

"What if it takes another month? Or more? How long do you
think it'll be before he kills some of the Plug-Uglies? Or even
some Orange-Eyes?"

"If I stay," I said, "maybe I can be a moderating influence.
If I leave with you, I'll feel I've signed half a dozen death war-
rants."

Kip leaned back on his camp chair and glared at Markham's
tent.

"Maybe we'd all be better off if he had a hunting accident,"
he mused.

"Then you'd be no better than him," I said.

"Sure I would," he replied. "I'd stop killing with one victim."

"I don't know. Sometimes it's harder to stop killing than
you think."

"Spare me your platitudes!" snapped Kip. "This man is in-
volving us all in his obsession, and he doesn't care who he kills
in the process." He paused. "Why are we doing this anyway?
Does anyone besides Markham seriously believe Drake has
found the cure to ybonia and has decided to keep it a secret?" He
turned to me. "Do *you?*"

"No," I admitted. "No, I don't."

"Then what difference does it make whether we find him
or not?"

"In terms of curing ybonia, probably none," I answered. "But in terms of keeping the Plug-Uglies and the Orange-Eyes alive, it could make a huge difference." I stared right back at him. "Now let me ask *you* a question: What do you suppose will happen if we desert?"

" 'Desert' isn't the word I'd use."

"Maybe not," I said. "But it's the word Markham will use, and the word ten billion people will identify us with. Do we really need that?"

"Shit!" he said. "I hadn't considered that."

"Well, you'd better *start* considering it."

Suddenly all the anger and tension seemed to leave his body. "So we stay," he said at last.

"We stay," I agreed.

"Someday I'll kill him."

"Not soon."

"No. First we find Drake. Then we get back to Fort Capstick. Then we part company. And then, someday, years from now, when he's least expecting it . . ."

"If you do it, backshoot him," I said.

"No. I've got to look him in the eye. He has to know who's doing it."

"If you let him see you, it won't be *you* who walks away when it's over."

"Thanks for your confidence," said Kip sullenly.

And suddenly I had no more desire to be in his company than in Markham's. I looked around, couldn't see Rashid or the cameramen anywhere, and walked off to my bubble. I lay down on my cot and spent the next hour thinking very troubled thoughts before I finally drifted off.

22

They say trouble begets more trouble. We begat more than our share the next afternoon.

We had been proceeding in a southerly direction, looking for the Orange-Eye village Ponta had told us about. It was a hellishly hot day, and since we were still paralleling the river it was very humid as well. Insects bit at our skins, thornbushes tore our clothes and flesh as we walked by, and at one point we came to the maggot-covered carcass of a dead Landwhale that had been rotting—and stinking—for days. The stench was enough to make half our party start vomiting.

We passed the Landwhale at midday, and since no one felt very hungry Markham drove us hard, deciding to skip lunch and see if we could make an extra six or seven miles.

"It can't be much farther," he remarked in midafternoon. "We've been traveling for eight days now. We ought to see a sign of them any time now."

Almost as if on cue, we *did* see a sign, as an arrow thudded home into the chest of one of the Plug-Uglies, who screamed and fell over. He was dead before he hit the ground.

"Take cover!" yelled Markham, which was a pretty useless thing to yell in the middle of a tropical forest, but within a few seconds we were all crouching behind trees and bushes, looking futilely for the enemy. Nothing happened for another five or six minutes. Then one of our Orange-Eyes stepped out onto the trail to try to spot who had attacked us, and got an arrow in the throat for his trouble.

Markham fired his laser pistol at the spot where the arrow had come from, and succeeded only in setting a tree on fire. Within minutes, a dozen more trees were blazing away, and our position was getting more precarious by the second.

"Big Shoulders!" I yelled. "Tell them we're friends, god-dammit!"

The Orange-Eye yelled something, and there was a reply a moment later.

"What did he say?" I demanded.

"Don't know!" shouted Big Shoulders from his place of hiding. "Not same language!"

"What the hell do they want?" I muttered, peering into the foliage, looking for an alien face, *any* face, that I could shoot at.

"You're not using your head," said Markham, scanning the terrain for the enemy.

"Okay," I said angrily. "What do *you* think they want?"

"Isn't it obvious?" he said. "They want to kill our Plug-Uglies."

"What makes you think so?" I asked, shooting at a flicker of motion and doing nothing more than killing an avian that was flying away from the growing fire.

"If Michael Drake has come this way, they have no reason to hate Men—and if he hasn't been here, they've never even seen a Man. They're Orange-Eyes; they have no reason to kill *our* Orange-Eyes. The Plug-Uglies live a few hundred miles away.

They've probably fought wars in the past. And the first arrow was aimed at a Plug-Ugly."

I didn't buy it. They could just as easily have been very territorial, and more than willing to kill Men, Plug-Uglies, Orange-Eyes, Dabihs, or any other beings that wandered in. But between the sporadic arrows that came our way and the raging fire that threatened to surround us, I didn't feel like wasting my time arguing.

"If we give them the Plug-Uglies, my bet is that they'll leave us alone," continued Markham.

"You can't do that," I said. "It would be murder."

"I'm open to suggestions," he replied. "But make them fast, before we're totally surrounded by this goddamned fire. Have you got a better idea?"

"If you're sure all they want are the Plug-Uglies, tell the Plugs to leave their packs and head off for their village. Maybe they'll leave us alone when they see we mean them no harm, and at least some of the Plug-Uglies will have a chance to get away alive."

"It *could* divert some of the bowmen," said Markham thoughtfully. "They'd concentrate on the Plug-Uglies while we make our way to the river."

"That wasn't what I had in mind," I said furiously. "Let's do our best to cover the poor bastards and give them a chance to escape. They don't have any weapons, and they're a couple of hundred miles from home."

"We protect Men first, and everyone else second," shot back Markham. "Cover my ass while I go talk to the Plugs."

He crawled on his belly until he reached the spot, some fifty yards away, where the Plug-Uglies were clustered. A moment later the entire lot of them broke and ran, with Markham shouting encouragement (and thus directing the attention of the enemy toward them). A moment later we could hear the local

Orange-Eyes racing through the forest, trying to run down the fleeing Plug-Uglies.

"That should buy us five minutes or so," said Markham, rejoining me.

"How did you talk them into leaving the only protection they had?" I asked.

"I told them that this wasn't their war, and I wanted those who made it all the way back to their village to tell Ponta that we sent them home rather than make them fight our battle." He grimaced. "I doubt that any of them will survive, but if they do, it's not a bad story to tell Ponta, just in case we have to pass through on the way back."

I saw another motion, used my Screecher, and saw an Orange-Eye fall out of a tree a quarter of a mile away.

"Nice shot," commented Markham.

"You were wrong," I said. "The Plug-Uglies are gone, and they *still* want to kill us."

"Well, it made sense," said Markham with a shrug. "Can't be right every time." He dismissed the Plug-Uglies from his thoughts. "Tell Mr. Ngami to stop using his Screecher and to go back to firing his Burner."

"You've got to be kidding!" I said. "We're in the middle of a forest fire."

"Not for long," said Markham. "Pass the word that on my signal, we're heading for the river. The Orange-Eyes and Dabihs will have to carry double loads."

"We'll be sitting ducks!" I protested.

"Anyone who gets in our way will be roasted ducks," he replied. "Tell Mr. Ngami to sweep the area with his Burner, and you do the same. I'm going to start right now."

He edged around a tree and fired his laser weapon, a long steady burst, and suddenly everything that hadn't been burning before was on fire. Kip and I did as he instructed. There were a few shrieks from within the inferno, though most of the enemy were positioned elsewhere.

When the fire and smoke got thick enough so that visibility was almost nil, Markham gave the signal.

"Now!" he shouted, and raced off toward the river, which was perhaps a quarter of a mile to our left.

I signaled Kip to wait until all of our party had taken off. Then, side by side, we trotted toward the river, sweeping the area with our laser pistols and adding to the conflagration.

When we finally reached the river, we found Markham and the others waiting for us.

"Why are you still here?" I asked.

"We've got a problem," said Markham.

"What is it? The river's only about fifty feet wide."

"But it's ten feet deep in the middle, and Big Shoulders just told me that Orange-Eyes can't swim."

I looked back at the wall of smoke. "Well, we can't just stand here," I said. "They'll pick us off one by one at their leisure."

"I've got an idea!" said Kerr suddenly. He pulled a tripod out of his camera kit and opened it up. The legs were each about eight feet long when fully extended. He raced to Arnaz's pack, pulled out another tripod, and opened it as well. "Get me something to connect them, and we've got something even stronger than a thirty-foot rope."

Arnaz produced some wire and began binding the two tripods together.

"Good idea!" said Markham. "Can the Dabihs swim?"

One of them assured him they could.

"Okay, then," said Markham. "I want two of you Dabihs to cross over to the other side of the river. Stay about waist deep, and take one end of the tripods with you. Two more get in waist deep on this side, and secure the other end of the tripods."

As they waded in, he gave Big Shoulders his orders.

"Each Orange-Eye will walk into the river, grab the tripod,

and pull himself, hand over hand, to the other side," he said. "Do you understand?"

Big Shoulders nodded and began explaining the plan to the Orange Eyes.

"Dr. Rashid!" called Markham. "Can you swim?"

"Yes."

"Is your bag waterproof?"

"The bag itself isn't, but everything inside it is in airtight safety containers."

"Okay, then go."

Rashid started making his way across the river.

Markham turned to the cameramen. "I know your stuff is safely packed. Any problem getting it across?"

"No," they replied in unison.

Markham took a close look at Arnaz, whose face was pretty badly disfigured. "Jesus, you look awful!"

"It's just some fungus," replied Arnaz. "I've had it for weeks."

"For weeks?" said Markham, surprised. Then he shrugged. "All right, get moving."

As the cameramen entered the water, he directed Kip and me to start firing random bursts into the smoke while he supervised the progress of the Orange-Eyes. All but two of them followed Big Shoulders' instructions and began slowly, carefully, making their way across the river. The last two cast terrified glances at the water and refused to join their companions.

"Big Shoulders!" snapped Markham.

"Yes?" said the Orange-Eye.

"Tell them to get into the water."

"They afraid."

"Tell them I'm not going to ask again."

Big Shoulders said something to them, they answered, and he turned to Markham. "They say you go, they stay and fight forest Orange-Eyes."

Markham pointed his pistol at the two terrified Orange-Eyes, fully prepared to kill them on the spot.

"Wait!" I said.

"What for?"

"You won't help our situation by shooting them down in cold blood," I said. "If they're really willing to fight the enemy, send them into the smoke and see if they can do some damage and buy us some time."

"Good idea," he agreed promptly. "Big Shoulders! Tell them to go after the forest Orange-Eyes or I'll kill them right where they stand!"

Big Shoulders relayed the message, and the two porters, looking only minimally less terrified of the enemy than of the water, cautiously approached the dense curtain of smoke, and vanished inside it.

There was a moment of total silence, then another. And then we heard a scream of agony, followed a few seconds later by a second one.

"All right, gentlemen," said Markham, making sure that all the other members of our party were safely across the river. "Swim for your lives!"

We all plunged into the water. Kip and I sidestroked across, holding our weapons aloft with our free hands. Markham just swam and didn't worry about how wet his got.

We heard alien war cries as we were climbing ashore on the far side of the river. Some fifteen or twenty of our Orange-Eyes and two of the Dabihs fell to the ground, impaled by spears and arrows, and we turned to see perhaps two hundred Orange-Eyes standing on the opposite shore, yelling and waving their weapons threateningly.

"Mr. Ngami, Mr. Stone, fire at will."

Kip and I turned our pistols on the Orange-Eyes, who obviously had never encountered sophisticated weaponry before and still hadn't connected the fire with them. They just stood there, screaming imprecations at us, while we mowed them down. They fell by the dozen, then by the hundred, and before a minute had passed the last of them lay twitching and smoldering on the opposite shore.

"What's the total here?" asked Markham as Rashid looked up from one of the dead Dabihs.

"Thirteen Orange-Eyes and two Dabihs dead," said Rashid. "I think I can patch up the other four Orange-Eyes—if you'll allow me to."

"Of course I will," snapped Markham. "Why do you ask?"

"You didn't always feel that way," said Rashid defensively.

"I had other options then. Now I don't. This is the team that finds Michael Drake or dies trying."

I looked across the river and saw some Plug-Ugly heads stuck on the ends of the Orange-Eyes' spears. Somehow I didn't feel like pointing out that more than half of us had *already* died trying, and we had no proof that we were any closer to Michael Drake than on the day we set out to find him.

23

We turned inland from the river, and the next two days passed without incident. Then, just as we were starting to feel safe once more, the Orange-Eyes attacked again.

We held them off thanks to our superior weaponry, but in the process Arnaz took an arrow in the leg and we lost five more of our own Orange-Eyes.

That night Arnaz's leg swelled up to twice its normal size, and he kept floating into and out of consciousness.

"Poison?" asked Markham as Rashid changed dressings on the wound.

"Definitely. But not one I've seen before. Probably made from some local plant."

"What's the prognosis?"

"If we were in the Democracy, or even back at Fort Capstick, I could save the leg. Out here, under these conditions . . ." He shrugged. "Who knows?"

"*I* need to know, damn it!" snapped Markham. "How soon before he can travel?"

"Weeks, if ever," replied Rashid.

"That's unacceptable. We can't afford to lose that much time—and besides, we're sitting ducks if we stay here." He stared down at Arnaz. "Maybe we can rig a litter and let a couple of Orange-Eyes carry him."

"They're already carrying close to triple loads," I noted. "I don't think they can manage a litter."

"For Arnaz's sake I hope you're wrong," said Markham. "Half a galaxy is waiting for us to find Michael Drake and bring him back. We can't lose any more time."

"Maybe we'll get lucky and be attacked six or seven more times," I said caustically. "*That* ought to keep your readers happy."

"I don't find that amusing, Mr. Stone," he said coldly.

"Neither do I," I shot back.

He ignored me and called to Big Shoulders. "Make a litter so that two of our porters can carry Mr. Arnaz."

It took a while to make the Orange-Eye understand what was required, but eventually he grasped what Markham wanted and ordered our Orange-Eyes to begin assembling something to carry Arnaz.

The next morning we set out in a southerly direction again, and within an hour we found ourselves under renewed attack. By this time the enemy had learned the range and power of our weapons, so they refused to show themselves. We would march, and after a few moments an arrow would fly toward us from the foliage a few hundred feet away. Sometimes it hit one of us, usually it didn't; but either way, there would be no repeat of it for five or ten minutes. Then, just as we began to relax and hope we had passed beyond their territory, another arrow would fly at us from a new hiding place.

When our third Orange-Eye fell to the ground with an arrow

piercing his neck, Big Shoulders shouted something in his own dialect and we came to a halt.

"What now?" demanded Markham as the burly Orange-Eye approached us.

"No more," said Big Shoulders.

"No more *what?*"

"No more carry for you, no more work for you. This is my world. You are the intruder. But who gets killed? Orange-Eyes. We go home now."

"You signed on for the whole trip!" said Markham heatedly.

"Agree to work for Kenny Vaughn, not for you," said Big Shoulders. "Kenny tells us to come back, we come."

"I'll kill any Orange-Eye that tries to leave!" snarled Markham, drawing his Burner. He glared at Big Shoulders. "You know I'm a man of my word."

The Orange-Eye stood there, not quite sure what to do next, when the matter was taken out of his hands. Half a dozen arrows streaked toward us, killing yet another Orange-Eye and one of our two remaining Dabihs. Markham, Kip, and I began firing our own weapons into the bush. We couldn't see the enemy, but we knew they were there. We exchanged fire for perhaps five minutes, and soon the forest around them was burning brightly, throwing great clouds of black smoke into the sky.

"*Shit!*" said Markham suddenly.

"What is it?" I asked. "Are you hit?"

"No, I'm not hit!" he grated. "Those bastards ran off and deserted while we were under attack!"

I looked around. Not a single Orange-Eye remained. All that was left were Markham, me, Kip, Rashid, the two cameramen, and one Dabih.

"So what do we do now?" asked Kip.

"We find Michael Drake, of course."

"With no porters and no supplies?" asked Kip. "Without even a bubble—unless you think you can carry one, toilet and shower included, all by yourself?"

"More to the point," said Kerr, "there's no radio. They took both units with them."

"They didn't want me to report them to Fort Capstick," said Markham. "Well, if they think we're going to curl up and die just because we haven't got porters, they don't know very much about Robert H. Markham."

"Then you plan to continue?" said Kip disbelievingly.

"We have no choice—the radio's gone. Besides, he's *here*, Mr. Ngami, and I intend to find him and bring him back! Nothing's changed."

"What the hell do you mean, nothing's changed?" demanded Kip. "We've just been deserted in the middle of an alien planet, surrounded by hostile natives. One member of our party can't even walk. Whatever we leave behind, whether it's foodstuffs or medical equipment or weaponry, we're going to find ourselves needing it before long." He stuck his chin out belligerently. "Name one thing that hasn't changed."

"*You* haven't, Mr. Ngami," said Markham. "You bitch and you threaten and you challenge, but when you're all through, you haven't the guts to carry out any of your threats. You're all noise and no action, and I'm getting tired of you."

"You listen to me—" began Kip furiously.

"No, I'm all through listening to you," said Markham. "Leave or stay as you wish. What you do doesn't interest me."

Kip glared at him. For a moment it looked like he was going to take a swing at Markham, but Markham had read him right. He was all talk and no action, and after another moment he sighed heavily and sat down with his back to a tree.

"All right," said Markham. "Our most pressing problem is Mr. Arnaz. Can we carry him?"

"We'll have to," I said. "You can't just leave him here."

"I could if Dr. Rashid volunteered to remain with him," answered Markham, staring meaningfully at the medic.

"So we can both be turned into pincushions ten minutes after you leave?" snapped Rashid. "Forget it!"

"I could leave you some weapons. You could try to catch up with us once he recovers."

"*If* he recovers," Rashid corrected him. "Besides, I don't know how to use your weapons, and Mr. Arnaz is in no condition to."

"All right, then," said Markham. "We carry him to the next friendly village."

"You know how long it's been since we've seen a *friendly* village?" asked Kip. "And he's one of us. You're not leaving him the way you left Stuart."

"What do *you* suggest?" asked Markham.

"We carry him until he can walk, of course."

"What do we leave behind?"

"Start with his camera equipment. It must weigh close to seventy-five pounds."

"What good's a cameraman without his camera?" demanded Markham.

"What good's a camera without a cameraman?" shot back Kip. "Besides, he's in no condition to use it."

"Enough arguing," I said. "There's a bunch of loads here. We'd better start figuring out what we *have* to take with us, and what we can leave behind."

"First intelligent thing I've heard since those fucking wags deserted," said Markham. He began walking from one load to the next.

"Are you sure we have time for this?" asked Kip, casting a nervous glance in the direction from which the arrows had come.

"They can't see through all that smoke any better than we

can," answered Markham. He looked at the various loads. "We'll do without the bubbles, of course. And the camp chairs. Ditto the irradiated food." He opened up a box. "Jesus!" he exclaimed. "We've been carrying tools for repairing the vehicles for how long?"

"Maybe we'd be better off deciding what we need, rather than what we don't," suggested Kerr.

"Fine," said Markham. "You're in charge of all your camera equipment. Can you handle anything else?"

"I can take a couple of sidearms."

"They're yours," said Markham. "Dr. Rashid, can you carry anything besides your medical kit?"

"Maybe a torch or two."

"That's all?"

"The kit's heavy."

"All right," said Markham. "Put the kit on the litter with Arnaz. You and the Dabih are in charge of it." He paused for a moment. "I'll take my computer and all my notes, a couple of sidearms, and a laser rifle. Let's see." He looked around. "I'll take the water purifiers. Which reminds me: Everyone fill your canteens now, and each of you take a purifying pellet from me. I don't plan to follow the river anymore. We're such a small party now that it'll just invite more attacks. And since we won't have any bubbles, we'll each take a bedroll." He turned to me. "Mr. Stone, you and Mr. Ngami go through all those packs and take only what's necessary—and I consider batteries for recharging your Burners and Screechers the most necessary items of all. You have half an hour."

Kip and I rummaged through the abandoned packs, picking out those things we felt we couldn't do without—extra batteries, a spare compass, more weaponry, spare boots (ours were practically falling apart), flares, insect repellents, a small hatchet for firewood, and various other items.

Finally we were ready, and we began marching. Markham

constantly pulled far ahead of us, but Kip, Kerr, and I had decided not to let Rashid and the Dabih fall behind. We were still in hostile territory, and we all felt that if we got even one hundred yards ahead of them, we might never see them again. At least, not alive.

We only made about six miles the rest of the day—we were just too heavily loaded down—but at least there were no more attacks. When we stopped for the night, we began reducing our packs. It was a pretty dismal site, that camp, filled with small biting insects, and at least two miles from water. It got cold after sunset, but we didn't dare light a fire that might attract the hostile Orange-Eyes, so we just sat there, shivering and miserable, trying to ignore the insects, listening for Redpanthers and other predators, kicking at the occasional snake that slithered toward us, attracted by our body heat.

To make things even worse, Arnaz developed a high fever and became delirious during the night. He finally fell asleep just before dawn. Then, when Rashid tried to wake him for breakfast a couple of hours later, he didn't respond. The doctor felt for his pulse, placed an ear next to the cameraman's chest, and finally announced that Arnaz had died from the poison.

While the Dabih dug a grave, the five remaining Men heated some coffee and dined on some bitter-tasting pink fruits.

"Our noble little party keeps getting nobler and littler," remarked Kip sardonically.

"That's a good line," said Markham admiringly. "I may borrow it."

"Well, I'm sure glad you got *something* out of his death," said Kip.

"What we got, if we are to be totally honest, is much greater mobility," replied Markham. "We should be able to make better than thirty miles a day with no litter to carry."

He then walked over to the grave, waited for Kerr to activate his camera, and delivered an eloquent eulogy that one day would bring tears to the eyes of five billion devoted viewers.

They were the most beautiful words and sentiments he ever voiced about the man who had risked his life time and again to help him obtain his stories. It was probably also the last time Markham ever gave him a thought.

24

We trudged on for another week before the Dabih vanished. Markham assumed he deserted. Kip thought he'd been nabbed by a Hooktooth or a Redpanther when he went off to get water. I felt it was just as likely that some stray Orange-Eye nailed him with a poisoned arrow. Whatever the truth of it, our party was now down to only five Men: Kenny Vaughn was dead, Arnaz was dead, Stuart was dead, and every Orange-Eye, Dabih, and Plug-Ugly was either dead or had deserted.

The most frustrating thing was that we'd lost the radios. Here we were, in the year 3322 of the Galactic Era, as completely out of touch with civilization as any ancient expedition back when Man was still Earthbound.

Markham was oblivious to our circumstances. He was here to find Michael Drake, and the more obstacles that were placed in his path, the greater would be his glory when he brought Drake back to the Democracy. So what if we were still subject to an occasional attack by the local Orange-Eyes? So what if a Red-panther, smelling the herbivore we'd killed and cooked, walked right up to our makeshift camp and got within ten feet of Rashid before Kip shot him? So what if Markham himself came down with a fever and was barely able to stand, let alone walk, for two days? It just meant he had that many more stories to sell.

Gradually the jungle became less dense, and before many days had passed we found ourselves in a green desert, a vast savannah that seemed filled with lush grasses and trees, but when we examined them more closely we found that they were all desert-adapted succulents. Water became very scarce. We were able to steal a few drops by cutting open some—but only some—of the plants and tubers we passed on our way. When we stopped at night we'd dig down four or five feet and wait for the groundwater to trickle in.

"You'd better find him quick," said Kip one evening as we sat in a circle around a small fire—we felt we were far enough from the Orange-Eyes' territory to chance it—and waited for the hole we'd dug to start producing water.

"Why this sudden enthusiasm?" asked Markham dryly.

"Because we've been out of contact with Fort Capstick for a couple of weeks," answered Kip. "They should be sending out a rescue party any day now."

"I doubt it," responded Markham.

"Why?"

"Because I've only contacted Fort Capstick four or five times since the expedition began. It's my readers who are used to encountering me on a daily basis, and since I was running some forty or fifty articles ahead, it'll be quite some time before they *stop* hearing from me."

"Well, then, your syndicate will be worried since they haven't heard from you."

"Not until we're down to the last four or five pieces," answered Markham. "They know I'm frequently out of touch for long periods of time."

"How comforting," muttered Rashid.

"We're getting close to him," said Markham. "I feel it in my gut."

"Once you find him, I hope to hell you think it was worth it," said Kip.

"Once I find him, the whole galaxy will think it was worth it," said Markham with absolute certainty.

Just then a huge Landwhale, the first we'd seen in months, appeared in the distance, followed by five more of its kind.

"Look at that male!" said Markham enthusiastically. "He must be a good twenty-one feet tall!"

The Landwhale suddenly lay down and rolled over in the dust, trying to rid its brown, layered skin of insects and parasites. It squealed with pleasure, then got back up.

"What a trophy he'll make!" said Markham.

"You don't have anyone to skin him or carry his various body parts," I noted.

"Why do you think I haven't shot him?" answered Markham. "But he'll make somebody a wonderful trophy." He paused, staring at the Landwhale. "Maybe even me. I wonder if Michael Drake can supply us with some porters?"

"Right," said Kip sarcastically. "Let's stop and do a little trophy hunting before presenting Man with a cure for ybonia."

Markham stared coldly at him, and finally spoke. "Mr. Ngami, for the longest time I thought that when I wrote my book, I would describe you as the ill-mannered malcontent that you are." He paused. "But now, upon further reflection, I don't think I'll mention you at all."

He got up and walked away, and Kip turned to me with a puzzled expression on his face. "Am I supposed to be shattered by that revelation?"

"From his point of view, yes," I said. "To Markham, there's no greater failure than the failure to leave a mark."

"Leave a mark?"

"To let someone know you were here, that you accomplished something with your life. That's his immortality, and by not mentioning you in his book and his articles and his video, he feels he can cost you yours."

Kip laughed. "He's crazier than I thought."

"You take your immortality any way you can get it," offered Kerr. "I go to church and pray when I'm back in civilization, and I make sure Markham writes me up when I'm out in the bush. Might as well cover all the bets."

"He'd better hope to hell that he's right about his kind of immortality," said Kip. "Because if it's the other kind, he's going to spend a long time roasting in hell."

"He'll have lots of company," said Kerr, unrolling his sleeping bag and climbing into it.

"I'll take the first watch," said Kip, pulling out his Burner.

"It's probably not necessary," I said. "I haven't seen any sign of Redpanthers or Hooktooths for a couple of days now."

"That's when they're most likely to kill you," he replied.

And sure enough, an hour later he nailed two Killerdogs that wandered into camp. The chorus from the rest of the pack kept us awake most of the night, and when we began walking the next morning we were all pretty bleary-eyed, which probably accounts for what happened next.

I can still see it in my mind's eye. Markham was leading the way, as usual, and Kerr was right behind him. I was bringing up the rear. The grass was sparse but knee-high, and suddenly Kerr started cursing.

"What's the matter?" asked Markham.

"I stepped in a pile of Landwhale shit!" muttered Kerr disgustedly.

"That'll teach you to watch where you're going," said Markham with a chuckle.

"How come *you* didn't step in it?" demanded Kerr.

"I stepped *over* it."

That was it. Just that simple. Kip and Rashid walked to their left to give the pile of dung a wide berth—and suddenly I couldn't see them anymore.

"Goddammit!" yelled Kip. "I think I broke my fucking leg!"

I rushed forward and saw that the ground had broken away and Kip and Rashid and fallen into a sinkhole. It had to be at least thirty feet deep, and they were up to their waists in water.

Suddenly Rashid shrieked.

"What is it?" I asked.

"Something *bit* me!" he hollered.

"Get the rope!" ordered Markham as he approached the edge of the sinkhole.

"I don't have it," said Kerr.

"Neither do I," I chimed in.

Rashid screamed again. "There's more than one of them!"

"*I've* got the rope!" yelled Kip. "It's in my backpack. Rashid, you've got to pull it out!"

But Rashid was screaming at the top of his lungs. "They're tearing me to pieces!"

Suddenly Kip yelped. "Jesus! There's something here with *teeth!*"

Markham started going through my pack and Kerr's, looking for anything that could serve as a rope.

The water was churning with activity, and Rashid was having trouble keeping his head about the surface.

"You've *got* to get the rope out!" ordered Kip. "It's our only chance!"

Rashid reached for Kip's pack—and suddenly realized that his hand was missing. He screamed again as blood spurted out, and then he vanished beneath the surface for the last time.

Kip had his laser pistol out, and started firing into the water. It boiled and bubbled and smoked, but we could see that whatever he was aiming at was still attacking him.

"Go away!" he yelled to us.

"We're looking for something to lower down to you!" I shouted.

"Forget it! I'm missing most of my leg, and the only guy who can fix it is dead! Just go! I'm about to lose it, and I don't want you watching when I do!"

And then he screamed, and screamed again, and kept on screaming as the water churned and turned a bright red. The screams grew weaker and weaker, and finally he went under and didn't come back up.

"God!" said Kerr with a shudder. "What a terrible way to die!"

"We packed the rope," I said dumbly. "How could we know that it would be with the guy who fell in?" I turned to Markham. "It's not our fault," I said, over and over again. "It's not our fault. We packed the rope. It's not our fault."

Finally he slapped my face. "Shut up! You're hysterical!"

"I'm sorry," I said, snapping out of it.

"We haven't got time for sorry," said Markham. "We've got to figure out what we've lost."

"Two men," I said dully.

"I mean, what was in their packs. We have to know what we're missing."

The three of us emptied our packs. We still had our weapons, and the water-purifying pellets and the hatchet, and we each had a bedroll. Kip had most of the batteries and charging units, which meant our weapons would be useless in a few more days, and of course Rashid had all the medications as well as the torches, which meant we wouldn't be able to see at night. One or the other also had all the insect repellents.

"All right," said Markham, when we'd completed our survey.

"We don't fire a shot from any of the weapons unless we're attacked and have no choice—and even then we wait until the
very last second so as not to waste any power. We're not going
to carry meat with us—that attracts predators—and I don't
want to run our weapons down shooting dinner every day, so
let's live on fruits, berries, and vegetation for as long as we can.
Somewhere in my computer I've got a list of every edible thing
on Bushveld, from tree barks to insects. I'll print it out on our
next break." He paused. "There's no sense turning back. Our
weapons would be useless long before we passed that Orange-
Eye territory, and who knows how the Plug-Uglies would react?
We're closer to Michael Drake than to any other safe haven on
the planet."

If he's alive, I thought grimly.

Finally he turned to Kerr. "I realize that everything happened too suddenly for you to capture it, but at least take some
footage of the sinkhole before we move on."

Kerr seemed about to protest, then shrugged, walked as
close to the edge as he dared, and held his camera out, pointing
it down to where Kip and Rashid had fallen. He kept it there for
half a minute, then backed up.

Markham approached the sinkhole, waited for Kerr to train
the camera on him, and offered the Lord's Prayer for his two
fallen comrades.

I noticed that Rashid was the only one he mentioned by
name.

25

The three of us walked silently for the rest of the day. Markham decided that to conserve our weapons' power packs, we should sleep in trees rather than take turns keeping watch against nocturnal predators. He had no problem, but Kerr and I kept rolling off our branches and falling painfully to the ground some ten feet below.

Finally I gave it up and stayed on the ground, sitting down and propping my back up against a tree. An hour later Kerr joined me, and from then on we elected to sleep on the ground. After all, a fully-charged weapon was no use to a man who'd just broken his neck falling out of a tree.

It was on the third day after losing Kip and Rashid that we came across the first positive sign of human life we'd seen. It wasn't much, to be sure, just a single footprint—but it was the print of a manufactured shoe, and I'd never known an Orange-Eye to wear shoes.

"It's *him!*" said Markham excitedly. "It's got to be! Who else could make a print like this?"

I couldn't argue with his conclusion, but neither of us had any idea how old the print was.

"It must be relatively fresh," insisted Markham. "Between the wind and the animals, I don't imagine it could last more than a day or two."

If Kenny had told me a footprint was less than two days old, I'd have believed him implicitly. But Markham wasn't any more of a tracker than I was, so I remained dubious.

"I'm telling you we're within a day of finding him!" said Markham.

"What direction will you go?" I asked. "All we have is this one print. Where was he going? When will he stop?"

"We'll go the direction it's pointing."

"That's not good enough," I said. "I've been watching you, and in the last half minute your feet have turned to every point on the compass. We don't have a set of tracks to show where Drake was walking. We have a single print. He could have turned to look in that direction, then turned back. I think we need something more to go on."

"Like what?"

"Instead of racing off hell for leather," I said, "let's spend a few minutes and see if we can hunt up some more footprints."

He agreed, and we began examining the uneven ground. I envied Kenny and his trackers their skill. I was sure any of them could spot a broken blade of grass, a thread from a jacket on a slender thorn, perhaps a bush that was leaning the wrong way, and be able to read the entire story: who had been here, how many were in the party, what where they doing, which way they were traveling, were they armed or unarmed . . . but try as I might, I couldn't come up with a thing. Not a print, not a sign, not anything.

"Any luck?" asked Markham after he'd covered his section of ground thoroughly.

I shook my head. "No."

He turned to Kerr. "How about you?"

"Outside of footprints, I don't even know what I'm looking for," answered the cameraman.

"Then I suggest we follow my original suggestion and head off in the direction the print is pointing."

"I have a better idea," said Kerr.

"I'm always open to suggestions," replied Markham. "What do you have in mind?"

"Let's shoot a couple of flares into the air. If he sees them, he'll find us a lot easier than we can find him."

"That's a very good idea," said Markham. "But the flares are in the bottom of the sinkhole with what's left of Mr. Ngami and Dr. Rashid."

"Then how about firing your projectile pistol?" continued Kerr. "It makes a pretty loud bang. Maybe he'll hear it."

"I don't know," said Markham. "It's the one weapon that can't run out of energy. I hate to waste any ammunition."

"If he hears it, it won't be a waste," I chimed in.

"He's an old man," said Markham, still uncertain. "What if he's hard of hearing? Or he's sleeping? Or standing near a waterfall?"

"Then he won't hear a damned thing, and we'll start walking again," answered Kerr. "But it's worth a try."

Markham frowned, trying to make a decision. Finally he withdrew his pistol from its holster, pointed it toward the sky, and fired it.

"A couple of more times," I said. "So he can't misinterpret it."

"As what?"

"I don't know—lightning, a falling tree, whatever. If you're going to do it, you've got to give it a chance."

He fired twice more.

"Are you satisfied now?" he said.

"Yes."

"So what do we do now?" continued Markham. "Make camp here and wait for him to find us?"

"No," I said. "We don't know he's heard it. If he doesn't give us a positive response, I think we'd better move on."

"With three bullets less in reserve," he said crankily.

"It was worth a chance."

Markham grimaced. "How the hell did you expect him to respond positively, even if he heard the shots?"

And just as the words left his mouth, we heard three answering shots.

"By God, it worked!" exclaimed Markham.

"So what do we do now?" asked Kerr. "Keep firing shots and hope we're getting closer?"

"I don't think so," I said. "He knows the area. We don't. We'll wait here for him."

"Not a fucking chance," said Markham. "We keep looking. I'm not going to have Kerr record me saying something like, 'We finally found you,' only to have him say, 'Nonsense—*I* found *you*.'"

"Will you at least fire a shot every few minutes so he'll keep answering?"

Now that he knew Michael Drake was nearby, Markham had no objection to spending some more ammunition, and we continued walking, certain that the object of our quest was finally within reach.

26

And finally, **many** months and many hardships and many lives after we had set out to find Michael Drake, we located him.

He was sitting on a crude wooden chair in front of an equally crude wooden house in the middle of a small compound. He was smoking a pipe and dressed in khaki. He wore a broad-brimmed straw hat that protected him from the sun.

He stood up when we made our way toward him, and I saw that he still had the thick mustache I had seen in Markham's photos and holos. The beard was gone, but that was the only difference. And he had the brightest, bluest eyes I'd ever seen.

The compound included a pair of outbuildings, plus a small hut on each side of his house. Suddenly five Orange-Eyes emerged from the huts and took up positions around him, staring at us distrustfully.

"It's all right," said Drake gently. "These are friends."

It was as simple as that. Four words and suddenly the surly Orange-Eye faces now bore happy welcoming smiles.

"Get that camera out!" whispered Markham, standing where he was until Kerr was ready to capture the scene for posterity.

When he was sure that the camera was running, Markham walked forward to Drake and extended his hand.

"My name is Robert H. Markham," he announced, articulating each word like a stage actor. "I thank God, sir, that I have finally found you."

"I am pleased to meet you," said Michael Drake, taking his hand. "But I'm really not lost, you know."

Kerr turned to me. "Should I stop?" he whispered.

"I think he'd kill you," I replied. "You can always edit it later."

He nodded and kept the holo camera going.

"But you have been missing for fifteen years, Dr. Drake," continued Markham, still speaking for posterity, "lost in this terrible wilderness."

"I am here by my own choice," answered Drake. "And I assure you I am not lost. In fact, I have mapped this entire area." He smiled again. "But where are my manners? You and your two companions must surely be hungry." He turned to one of the Orange-Eyes. "Gabriel, please show them where they can wash up, and then bring them to the dining room." Then to another. "Peter, there will be four for lunch."

He disappeared inside his cabin, Kerr deactivated the camera, and the three of us followed Gabriel to the first washbasin and soap I had seen in a very long time.

"Dr. Drake doesn't seem surprised to see us," remarked Markham to the Orange-Eye.

"He has known you were coming for many days," answered Gabriel in better Terran than any Orange-Eye I'd come across.

"Oh?" said Markham. "How?"

"You must ask him" was the reply. "I am only his servant."

"We'll need porters when we return to Fort Capstick. How much does Dr. Drake pay you?"

Gabriel smiled. "I would not accept payment from Michael Drake. None of us would."

"You wouldn't?"

"We should pay him for the privilege of his company." Gabriel turned and walked away. "I will wait outside for you."

"Well," I said when the three of us were alone, "he seems to be everything he's cracked up to be."

"Then why has he buried himself here for fifteen years?" shot back Markham. "There's more here than meets the eye."

"Or less," I replied. "I think he's exactly what he seems to be: a simple, saintly man."

"There's nothing simple about him," said Markham. "He's got a mind like a steel trap. He's the only man ever to win the Hazewell Prize twice—and he's the man who created the first ybonia vaccine."

"All right," I corrected myself. "He's a complex, saintly man."

"He's hiding," said Markham. "And I want to know what he's hiding *from*."

"How about journalists?" I suggested.

He stared at me for a long moment. "When this expedition is over," he said at last, "don't apply for a job as a humorist."

He finished washing his hands and stepped aside so that Kerr and I could get to the basin. When we were all through, we joined Gabriel, who took us to Drake's cabin.

The interior was very austere. A large cross of polished hard-wood—the first religious symbol I'd seen in years—hung over the fireplace. There was a single bookshelf, filled to overflowing, and I noticed that most of the books were falling apart, perhaps due to overuse, perhaps due to the humidity. When I looked closer, I was surprised to find they were not medical and scientific texts, but rather the Bible, the complete works of the Can-

phorian poet Tanblixt, a number of Shakespeare's plays, and
Homer's *Iliad* and *Odyssey*.

The door was open to the bedroom, and I saw it consisted of
nothing but a simple cot, a nightstand with a small reading
lamp, and a crude dresser. At the other end of the cabin was the
kitchen, where an Orange-Eye was making lunch.

There was a table set up in the main room, and Drake gestured us to sit down, then joined us.

"You look rather the worse for wear," he observed.

"We've been searching for you for a long time, sir," said
Markham.

"Why?"

"The ybonia virus has mutated."

"Yes, I know," said Drake. "That was my initial reason for
coming here: to find a cure for the new disease."

"Then shall we assume you haven't yet found it?" asked
Markham.

"Peter!" said Drake to the kitchen Orange-Eye. "I believe
we're ready to eat now." He turned back to us. "All our food is
locally grown. I assume you've consumed enough so that you
know whether or not you are allergic to any of it."

"We're all fine," Markham assured him. "Is there any
meat?"

"We don't believe in killing things here," said Drake as Peter
brought four large bowls of salad to the table. "There is a fruit—
the Orange-Eyes have an unpronounceable name for it—that
tastes very much like a lemon, and when squeezed and chilled
is almost identical to lemonade." Peter returned with four full
glasses. "I trust you will enjoy it."

"I don't see any source of power here," I noted. "How do you
manage to chill it?"

"The power plant's in my laboratory," replied Drake. He
smiled. "Since I don't have to share it with anyone, I keep all my
cold drinks in the lab's refrigerator."

"Are you close to a cure?" asked Markham.

"For lemonade or for refrigerators?"

"For ybonia," said Markham. "Or have you given up on it?"

"Let's say that I've given up."

Markham and I exchanged glances. I don't know what he was thinking, but I was curious about the very careful way Michael Drake worded his sentences whenever he spoke of ybonia. I didn't know what it meant, but it piqued my curiosity.

"I'd like to see your laboratory later," said Markham.

"I'll be very happy to show it off to you," replied Drake. "Though I'm sure it will appear more primitive than any laboratory you've ever seen."

Again, I was struck by his language: *appear* more, not *be* more. He wasn't going to lie to us, but it *felt* like he was going out of his way not to tell us the truth.

"Have you any batteries for recharging our weapons?" asked Markham.

"You won't need weapons here," said Drake. "We have no enemies."

"*You* may not," said Markham. "But *we* sure as hell do."

"No one will harm you while you're in my company."

"We're going to have to pass through the territory of some very hostile and aggressive tribes when we bring you back," continued Markham. "I don't think we can count on them to hold their fire just because you're with us."

"I'm not going anywhere, Mr. Markham," said Drake. "But I concede your point: before you leave, I shall allow you to recharge your weapons."

"What do you mean, you're not going anywhere?" demanded Markham. "We came here to rescue you and take you back to the Democracy."

"As you can see, I am in no need of rescue," explained Drake patiently. "As for the Democracy, I know how to find my way back to it should I ever want to. At the present time, I am quite content where I am."

"But that's crazy!" exploded Markham, frustrated. "Come back with us and I can set you up in the finest laboratory on Deluros VIII, with hundreds of assistants and unlimited funding."

"I don't doubt your word, Mr. Markham," said Drake, "but I am perfectly happy right here. My laboratory, simple as it is, is quite adequate for my needs."

"Don't you ever feel a need to talk to anyone?"

"I am surrounded by friends, and I talk to them all the time."

"Friends?" repeated Markham, puzzled.

"You've met two of them already—Peter and Gabriel—and you saw some of the others when you first arrived. Most live in their own villages a few miles away, but five of them have elected to remain here with me."

"But they're *wags!*"

"That's an ugly word, Mr. Markham," said Drake softly, staring at him with those penetrating blue eyes. "I am sure you meant no insult, but I must ask you not to utter it again."

"I apologize," said Markham quickly.

It seemed time for a change of subject, so I spoke up. "I was just admiring the lovely cross you have over your fireplace, Dr. Drake," I said.

"It took me more than a month to get the finish of the wood just right," he said with a note of pride.

"Have you converted any of the local Orange-Eyes?" I asked.

He shook his head. "I haven't even tried."

"Why not?"

"I have my beliefs and they have theirs. It would be ludicrous to try to convince an Orange-Eye that Jesus died half a galaxy away and six thousand years ago for his sins."

"What *have* you taught them besides our language?"

"Simple medical procedures. When I arrived, they put their health in the hands of the local—what shall I call him? the local *shaman*—who prescribed for them by the equivalent of rolling bones in the dirt." He paused thoughtfully. "Although some of the herbs and cures he prescribed did indeed have some beneficial effects on the Orange-Eyes' metabolism. Anyway, now they know how to treat simple diseases, how to set fractures, how to create certain antibiotics, and, perhaps most important, they know the basics of hygiene and sanitation. I am sure you noticed that I have two outbuildings here. One, as I said, is my laboratory, and the other is my hospital. I am proud to say that the hospital has been completely empty for months."

"Well, that's certainly encouraging," said Markham.

"I have also taught them—or *tried* to teach them, at any rate—the sanctity of all living things."

"I wish you'd taught some of the Orange-Eyes and Plug-Uglies north of here."

"Plug-Uglies?"

Markham briefly described Ponta's race.

"Ah!" exclaimed Drake. "You are referring to the People." He paused. "They do not consider themselves ugly, and neither do I."

"They look like they've all got skin diseases."

"They live in thick bush. Their skin must be hard so that they're not constantly cutting it against thorns and limbs."

"Couldn't it look hard without looking like it has infections and eruptions all over it?" asked Markham. "They look like open, oozing sores."

"What oozes out of those eruptions is a natural insect and parasite repellent," replied Drake with a smile. "Your journey would doubtless have been much more comfortable if you'd had those same eruptions protecting *your* skin."

"I had no idea," admitted Markham.

"Somehow I'm not surprised," said Drake. He paused. "Perhaps when you leave tomorrow morning, I will give you each a container containing the essence of the People's repellent."

"Who says we're leaving tomorrow morning?" asked Markham promptly, almost pugnaciously.

"I do," answered Drake. "I am happy to feed you and offer you shelter after your long ordeal, but I did not ask for your company and I do not desire it."

"You haven't liked me from the moment I got here," said Markham. "Why? What have I ever done to you?"

"Nothing," admitted Drake.

"You are an extraordinary man," continued Markham. "Why should you resent the fact that another extraordinary man has given a year of his life to find you and bring you back to civilization, where your gifts can be put to the greatest use?"

"I do not resent the fact that you are extraordinary," said Drake. "I resent the fact that you are not."

"The hell I'm not!" Markham retorted angrily. "Who else could have put this expedition together and found you?"

"I've no idea," answered Drake, his penetrating blue eyes belying the gentleness of his voice. "But very little goes on in the bush that I'm not made aware of. You whipped one of your Orange-Eyes. You killed two of the People before they would agree to be your porters, and you turned the porters into cannon fodder to escape a tribe of Orange-Eyes whose territory you invaded. Your aggression has caused the deaths of many People and Orange-Eyes and Dabihs. The intelligent ones, the lucky ones, deserted before you could get *them* killed too. While claiming the highest of purposes, you have made war on the races of this planet." He continued staring at Markham. "No, Mr. Markham, you are an absolutely ordinary Man, and that is why I have washed my hands of your race and chosen to live out my life on Bushveld, trying in my own small way to make amends to two of the thousands of races we have brutalized since leaving our home planet."

"That's your final word?" said Markham bitterly. "You won't come back with us?"

"Haven't you been listening?" replied Drake, and for the first time he allowed his irritation to creep into his voice.

"Well, all I can say is that it's a goddamned shame," said Markham. "With the money and the help I could have obtained for you, you might have actually come up with a cure in four or five years."

And now, before he could hide it, I thought I could spot just the tiniest touch of arrogance in Drake's voice. "What kind of incompetent do you take me for, Mr. Markham?" he demanded.

"What are you talking about?" demanded Markham, puzzled.

"I solved the ybonia problem six months after I arrived here."

27

For a long moment nobody said a word. We just sat there, stunned. Finally Markham spoke up.

"Are you saying that you've had a cure for ybonia for more than a decade, and you haven't told anyone about it?"

"That is correct, Mr. Markham."

"Do you know how many men have died of it during that time?" demanded Markham.

"A drop in the bucket, compared to the number of aliens we've killed or pacified," responded Drake. "And by 'pacified,' which is the Navy's rather euphemistic term, I mean, of course, brutalized, dominated, enslaved, or exterminated."

"What the hell has one got to do with the other? You've got the means to save literally hundreds of millions of your own kind!"

Drake stared at him placidly. "You are not my own kind, Mr. Markham. I cured the People; you enslaved and murdered them. I have taught the Orange-Eyes; you have merely used them until they died or deserted. The galaxy will be none the poorer for having a hundred million less of you around."

Now Kerr spoke up for the first time. "My mother died of ybonia," he said. "*She* wasn't like him."

"Then I'm sorry," answered Drake. "But I'm sure there are tens of thousands of scientists working on the cure. They'll come up with it one of these days. It's really not that complicated."

"Bullshit!" grated Markham. "That's like Einstein saying that the theory of relativity wasn't that complicated. Maybe not, but it took the race more than a million years to produce a man who could dope it out!"

"You flatter me."

"Flatter you?" exploded Markham. "I'd like to tie you up and drag you back to civilization! You owe it to Man to tell us what you discovered."

"Man is well ahead of the game," said Drake calmly. "No one owes him anything. Least of all me. I've already given the race a vaccine that protected hundreds of billions, or have you forgotten that?"

"That doesn't free you from your obligation to save us again!"

"I have been waiting for all my adult life for the race of Man to give me a single sign that it's *worth* saving," replied Drake with genuine sadness. "When I realized that it would never do so, I dedicated my remaining years to working with more deserving races."

Markham pulled out his laser pistol. "What if I promise to kill you if you refuse to come back with me?"

Drake smiled. "Then you will be a murderer, and for no gain, because if I will not reveal the formula to you while I am alive, I most certainly cannot do so after I'm dead." He paused. "Now put your weapon away, or I will insist that you use it."

"You're right," said Markham thoughtfully. "I can't kill you." He turned and aimed the pistol at Peter, who was preparing dessert in the kitchen. "But I can kill off your Orange-Eyes one at a time until you agree to cooperate."

Drake signed deeply, then closed his eyes and shook his head. "My brief association with you has only strengthened my resolve. I cannot and will not help you keep more conquerors alive. Do what you will with my friends and myself. God will punish you soon enough."

Markham glared at him for a long moment, then holstered his weapon.

"I foot-slogged across thousands of miles of this godawful planet to find a saint," he said bitterly. "What I found was a traitor."

"If you say so," replied Drake mildly.

"I plan to say so," snarled Markham. "And five billion people will be listening!"

"Say what you will," answered Drake with a shrug. "If their opinions mattered to me, so would their lives."

"They don't deserve to die because you're justifiably upset with Markham and his ilk," I said, ignoring Markham's furious glare.

"Many don't," admitted Drake, "and that saddens me. But the cure is as unselective as the disease, and I must spend my remaining efforts on helping the local races before their progress is thwarted and their freedoms curtailed by the Robert Markhams of the galaxy."

"I'll make you a deal," said Markham. "Give me the cure, and you can not only stay here, but I'll make you out to be a hero, working to save the Orange-Eyes from some epidemic now that you've saved your own people."

"I don't believe you've heard a word I've said," replied Drake. He got to his feet. "Gentleman, I expect you to leave at sunrise."

Then he walked out into the night.

28

A hand shook me awake in the middle of the night.

"What the hell is—?" I began.

The hand clamped down on my mouth.

"Quiet!" whispered Markham.

I sat up, and saw Kerr was standing groggily.

"What's going on?" I whispered.

"Come with me," said Markham.

He waited until I was on my feet and then led Kerr and me out of the guest hut in which we'd been sleeping. We walked silently around to the back of Michael Drake's compound, and finally came to the door of a wooden building.

"Follow me," whispered Markham, carefully opening the thick door. It squeaked slightly, and he held still until we were sure no one had been awakened. Then we opened it the rest of the way and entered the building.

"What is this place?" I whispered.

He hit a switch, and suddenly three small lights came to life. I looked around and realized we were in Drake's laboratory. The equipment wasn't up to Democracy standards, but it seemed in good working order. There were beakers, test tubes, a pair of microscopes—one molecular, one electron—and a large number of batteries and chargers of all sizes. Thousands of local plants were carefully stored and labeled. I opened the door of his refrigerator and found blood samples, also all neatly labeled, right next to the mock lemonade.

Then I saw the radio.

"The power module's glowing," I noted.

"It's been on for a while," answered Markham. "I've already contacted Governor Penner back at Fort Capstick, and his people are homing in on our signal. They should be able to fly in a rescue party by tomorrow morning."

"Michael Drake's not going to be happy about that," I pointed out. "He wants to stay undiscovered."

"There's a *lot* he's not going to be happy about," said Markham. He held up a small, sparkling cube.

"What's that?" asked Kerr.

"Everything his computer had on ybonia," answered Markham. "Notes, observations, formulas, everything. It's all encrypted, but I'm sure there are men and women on Deluros who can break the code."

"You're really going to steal it?" said Kerr.

"Absolutely," he replied. "Think of the tens of millions of lives it'll save."

"I didn't think you cared about them any more than Drake does," I remarked.

"I don't," said Markham. "But my story's got to have an ending. Michael Drake's a hero, whether he wants to be or not, and the galaxy needs all the heroes it can get."

"And what about Drake himself?" I asked.

"Yes," said a voice from behind us. "I'm rather curious my-self. What about me?"

We spun around and found ourselves facing Michael Drake, who stood in the doorway.

Markham placed the cube in one of his many pockets. "I'm taking this back with me."

"I suppose after all those murders a little thing like theft wouldn't bother you at all," said Drake.

"Theft?" repeated Markham. "Hell, *you* stole Man's future. I'm just giving it back."

"I am always amazed at the power of the human mind to ra-tionalize," replied Drake. "You are a thief and a killer, and I cannot let you leave with that cube."

"And just how does a pacifist propose to stop me?"

Drake looked at the glowing module on the radio. "I see that you're allowing Fort Capstick to home in on our signal. I as-sume you've asked for a rescue plane. When it arrives, I will ex-plain that you have stolen that which does not belong to you, and demand its return."

"And when I tell the pilot what it is, do you actually think he'll make me give it up?" asked Markham incredulously.

"No," admitted Drake slowly. "No, I suppose he won't." He paused and stared at the three of us. "Then I must find some way to stop you myself."

"Save your strength," said Markham. "You're outnumbered, and we've got all the weapons. Besides, no one wants to harm you. I'm still willing to make you the greatest hero in the Democracy if you'll do what I tell you."

"I have no interest in becoming your slave or your puppet," said Drake.

He reached for something in the shadows, and Markham immediately fired his laser. Drake screamed and fell to his knees, his left hand a charred, black, smoking ember, blood pouring out of his arm at the wrist, and a second ugly wound in his chest.

"What was he going for?" yelled Markham, never lowering his pistol. "A gun? Some toxic container?"

Kerr walked over, looked where Drake had been reaching, and withdraw a battered copy of the Bible.

Markham holstered his weapon and knelt down next to Drake.

"I told you I was a pacifist," mumbled Drake weakly, the red spot on his shirt growing larger by the second.

"You damned fool!" said Markham. "What was so fucking important that you had to reach like that?"

"Just a line of text," said Drake so softly we could barely hear him.

"What line?" I asked.

"Forgive them, Father, for they know not what they do," said Michael Drake, and died.

Markham stood up and stared at the corpse. "Stupid son of a bitch!" he said bitterly. "I could have made you bigger than God!" He paused. "I still can."

"What the hell are you talking about?" I demanded. "You just killed him."

"Keep your voice down!" snapped Markham. He looked hastily out the window to see if we'd awakened any of the Orange-Eyes. "There are picks and shovels over there," he said, pointing to a row of tools stacked neatly by the rear door. "Take him out back and bury him."

"But—"

"Get moving!" he ordered. "This is no time to argue!"

I liked to think that I was different from Kip, that he was a talker and I was a doer, but in times of crisis I tend to follow orders without thinking, and I did so again this time. Kerr and I carried the body out the back door of the lab, dug a shallow

grave as fast as we could, and laid him in it. We had just finished covering him when Markham appeared.

"All right," he said. "Let's give him the decent Christian bur-
ial he would have wanted."

"Now?" I asked, surprised.

He turned to Kerr. "Use your infrared lens."

"What about the Orange-Eyes?" I demanded, though I suddenly had a sinking feeling that I knew what the answer
would be.

"They won't bother us."

"You goddamned murderer!" I shouted furiously. "You
killed all five of them while we were burying Drake, didn't you?"

"I'm saving hundreds of millions of Men," he answered.
"It's a small price to pay."

"Why pay it at all?"

"They'd have torn us apart the instant they learned Drake
was dead."

"We could have left him in the lab," I said, trying to control
my temper. "They didn't have to know until after we were
gone." I glared at him. "What's the *real* reason?"

"I'm creating the greatest story in the history of journalism," said Markham without a trace of regret. "I won't allow a
bunch of illiterate aliens to talk to the rescue crew or anyone else
and fuck up the ending."

Then, as calmly as if nothing had happened, he stepped up
to the grave, pulled the Bible out of a pocket, found a touching
verse, and began reading over Michael Drake's grave.

Epilogue

Michael Drake died of ybonia. He had exposed himself to the deadly virus so often while attempting to find a cure that he finally contracted the dread disease. He worked night and day for as long as his diminishing strength would allow, and finally, almost unbelievably given his weakened condition, he discovered the cure. The remnants of our party arrived there the day before he died. His greatest fear had been that his research would die with him, but Robert Markham personally promised that he would deliver the formula to the Democracy, and despite unending hardship and terrifying battles against hostile aliens, Markham did just that. At least, that's what The Book said, and everybody believed The Book. It was entitled *Finding Michael Drake,* and it sold seven billion copies throughout the Democracy.

"I thank God, sir, that I have finally found you," became the single best-known utterance since "Let there be light!" Children on planets tens of thousands of light-years away fought for the right to pretend to be Robert Markham. The holo of Markham's first meeting with Drake won every award that could be given. (The critics marveled at how well Drake was able to hide his infirmities from the camera.)

The cure worked, of course. Michael Drake was as good as his press clippings. Within two years the vaccine—well, antidote, really—had been synthesized, mass-produced, and distributed to all half million of the Democracy's worlds, and no man would ever die of ybonia again.

That was the key. Despite everything else, despite the brutality and the hypocrisy and the lies, Markham *was* a hero. He'd done what even Michael Drake couldn't or wouldn't do: he went into the jungles of Bushveld and came out with the cure.

They were both touched by greatness, Markham and Drake, each in their separate ways. And given what their greatness led them to do, it made me happy that I was just a normal man without a shred of greatness in me.

I applied for my old job with the museum, the job I had once hated, and was thrilled when they agreed to take me back. Some time later Kerr stopped by my crowded little office. He was going off with Markham again, this time to rescue Ambassador Alicia Willows, who was reportedly a captive of the natives of Kennedy III. He left some holos and tapes on my desk without a word of explanation.

Later that night, in the privacy of my apartment, I looked at them. They included the whipping of the Orange-Eye, the murder of the People, even an audio tape made, without our knowledge, immediately after Michael Drake's death.

I realized that with one call to the press, I could destroy everything that Robert Markham had accomplished, expose the myth and the lies for what they were. I was ready to do so, too, but some inner instinct stopped me, and I filed my evidence away.

Years later Markham returned triumphantly with Alicia Willows at his side, and though I later found out from Kerr that she was never in any danger and indeed hadn't needed to be "rescued," the book sold another few billion copies and brought Markham even more fame for the hardships and privation his new team had undergone during the daring rescue.

I even bought a copy. And after I read it, I carefully tossed the book and the incriminating holos and tapes, one by one, into the atomizer. I wouldn't be a great man or a hero on a bet, but the galaxy needed greatness and heroes a lot more than it needed one more chronicle of Man's duplicity.

I allowed Robert Markham to remain both.